Praise for "The Expl

"*The Exploding Memoir* has the energy of hard boiled pulp delivered like a burst of feedback, spinning its tale of juvenile delinquency, petty crime, and mysterious missions against a background of the early seventies Californian counter culture and the inevitable turn towards punk."
 Jack Sargeant, author of *Flesh and Excess*, *Naked Lens*, etc

"Johnny Strike's mastery of Beat-tinged crime fiction is unequaled in my reading experience. I can highly recommend *The Exploding Memoir*."
 James Grauerholz
 Bibliographer and literary executor, William S. Burroughs estate

"*The Exploding Memoir* is yet another genre bending and transcending work by Johnny Strike. A work so underground that it's cthonic, it's also a thrilling ride that you don't want to miss."
 Michael A. Lucas, author of *Devil Born Without Horns*

"*The Exploding Memoir* is a tale delivered in Johnny Strike's engaging manner. Musicians, magicians, and easy money come together in a dangerous world that carries the cold ring of truth about it."
 David Kerekes, author *Mezzognorno Life, Death in Southern Italy*

"A compelling and intriguing title, written by an intriguing and compelling author. Johnny Strike has all the right influences — noir, pulp, punk, but like an alchemist (or a mutant mixologist) he combines and recombines elements until he comes up with a concoction that's uniquely his own."
 Geoff Nicholson, author of *Bleeding London*

"It begins as all sojourns do; relatively normal, but soon reveals a metaphysically jeweled magic carpet ride from The Fool in the Tarot Deck to a carefully plotted destiny no one ever suspects... Strike hums and vibrates with realistic characters that rise and fall within the unrestricted setting of the 1970s, peppered with Ancient Gods and Goddesses, and himself--the music that makes it all flow with a river of highly intelligent psychedelic adventure."
 Rain Graves, two-time winner of the Bram Stoker Award

The EXPLODING MEMOIR

JOHNNY STRIKE

boldventurepress.com

Other books by Johnny Strike

Ports of Hell

A Loud Humming Sound Came from Above

Name of the Stranger

Murder in the Medina

The Exploding Memoir
by Johnny Strike
July 2018

Scott Owen, editor
(aka John Marr, editor
of *Murder Can Be Fun*)

www.boldventurepress.com

"The Exploding Memoir ©2018 Johnny Strike. All Rights Reserved.

ISBN-13: 978-1721939107
Retail cover price $9.95
Available in eBook edition

All rights reserved. No part of this book may be reproduced or transmitted in any form or by any means without express permission of the publisher and copyright holder.

All persons, places and events in this book are fictitious, and any resemblance to any actual persons, places or events is purely coincidental.

Printed and bound in the United States.

Again,
for Jane

The EXPLODING MEMOIR

1

Harrisburg, Pennsylvania 1969.

Eddie picked up the phone. An anonymous voice said, "They're going to put you in reform school." The anonymous voice belonged to Mr. Patterson, Eddie's PO. "You'd better get out of town, and quick," the probation officer added.

"Thanks," Eddie said. "You've been terrific Mr. Patterson, best to you as well."

Eddie considered himself mighty lucky to have Mr. Patterson as a probation officer. Patterson had been fresh to the department, with the noble ideal to change the rotten, corrupt system. Patterson's father had belonged to system, until he was shot dead by a Puerto Rican kid he'd been harassing. Patterson hated his father, hadn't mourned his death at all. He wanted to do the opposite of his old man had done — but when he came aboard the Harrisburg, P.A. Juvenile Probation Department, he found they were all like his old man. He tried changing things from within, but after nearly two years decided it was useless, impossible. He would go back to law school at the end of the year.

Today he'd been informed that his caseload was being taken from him and he would be doing desk work for the foreseeable future. Still, while he was there he would do as much positive work as possible. Letting Eddie Knox know his superiors had plans to pick him up, put him in reform school for a year or two, that they would use probation violation technicalities to do so was one of those positive moves.

Patterson didn't think that Knox was a bad kid, only that he'd made some bad decisions, had a less than desirable upbringing, had drifted into the wrong crowd, and then got caught up in the Kafkaesque juvenile probation system. A year or two in reform school would only help to make Knox a career criminal. Maybe if he could get away, he would have a chance to change his life. Patterson was glad he had tipped him off.

Eddie called Neil Stanton, his English teacher at the community college and told him what was happening. Neil was an anti-government lefty who smoked pot, listened to Bob Dylan, and Pete Seeger, and protested the Vietnam war. He had taken Eddie to Harrisburg's one and only beatnik coffee shop for a poetry reading. Eddie enjoyed it, he too liked to smoke weed, and take acid. Neil had praised the short stories he'd handed in, but Eddie was too shy to consider reading one aloud outside of class. The two had also bonded because Eddie was friends with Allison, a student Neil was sleeping with. Neil was the only one Eddie could think of who could possibly help him out of this situation. He was right. Neil told him to wait at a bowling alley behind a local mall, out of sight. He would pick him up in an hour. Neil had a house about thirty minutes out of the city, nestled in a picturesque wooded area by a wandering stream.

Eddie decided that first he would chance to stop by his own studio apartment to pick up a few things. As he was turning the corner he saw his old probation officer, the uber prick Mr. Graham coming out of his building. Shit! Fuck! Shit! Eddie stepped behind a phone booth in the nick of time. Graham was a sadist. Eddie had thanked all the gods when he had been transferred to Patterson's caseload. However, there he was, back on Graham's caseload who was presently looking up and down the street. Was he sniffing the air like some kind of human animal? Eddie watched

Graham get into a black sedan that was driven by a stocky man with white hair: Mr. White, the head of the goddamn department. Still Eddie waited since they sometimes would circle the block, an old trick. They did. Only then did Eddie head toward his place. He made his visit quick. Coming out, he ran into the landlord who said someone was just by to see him: a Mr. Graham, and that Eddie was supposed to call him right away. The landlord gave him a funny look, handed him a number on an slip of paper. Eddie thanked him and to explain his packed bag, said he was going on a camping trip to the Blue Ridge Mountains.

Having some time to kill Eddie thought he would call Graham for a laugh. He used a pay phone on his way to the bowling alley. Graham wasn't back yet but the receptionist transferred his call to Graham's buddy Brauer, another asshole. He told Eddie in a phony friendly voice to come in for a "briefing" since he'd been switched back to Graham's caseload. "Strictly a formality," Brauer said mildly. "Sure, what time should I come in sir?" Eddie asked stifling a laugh. Brauer gave him an appointment for the following day at 9:30 AM. "Thanks Mr. Brauer I'll be there tomorrow then." Eddie was sure that Brauer would tell Graham, and add something like: "...and the schmuck has no idea you're gonna lock his ass up." They would both have a good laugh. Mr. White would bite into a jelly donut, wipe his rotten mouth and laugh as well.

Neil, who looked like a shorter, stockier version of John Lennon was right on time with his beat up green VW van that smelled of Richard, Neil's black lab named for the poet Richard Brautigan. Richard licked Eddie's ear until he turned around and gave the dog some vigorous rubs, and pushes.

"Hey, Richard remembers you." Neil wasted no time getting out onto the freeway. "Listen Eddie, don't you worry about a thing. They're not going to put you in any nazi reform school, because they won't be able to find you." Neil lit a joint, passed it to Eddie, and slid in an 8 Track of Donavan into the player.

"Let's hear some 'Mellow Yellow' and mellow you out; you're like a spring loaded weapon."

"Sorry, but I remember the last time they locked me up. I think I'd rather snuff it than go back to jail."

"Don't talk crazy, and don't worry. I have a magnificent plan already in the works. Are you ready for Cal-i-forn-i-a, the land of the free?"

"What? California? Yeah, I'd love to—"

"You have a ticket to San Francisco leaving in three days, out of Washington D.C. You can stay with my friends out there until you get on your feet. I might even be able to find you some work. I hope you keep at your writing, because that's your real escape, not this petty crime business."

"I'll pay you back, somehow," Eddie said, beginning to relax, as the pot high crept over him. He watched the farmlands rapidly passing by, full of emptiness, full of space, the leftover snow stained at the boundaries. Neil turned onto a less traveled road, then onto another. The area was like a picture out of *Field and Stream*. Neil's place was on a hillside overlooking a glistening, snaky creek with rocks above the surface here there, at points where you could walk across. A variety of trees populated the hilly area; no neighbors could be seen. Eddie felt safe from the grasp of the probation department now. The next three days he spent raising as much cash as he could from close friends via Neil. He discovered by phone that Graham had been to various places he frequented. He had questioned Benny, one of Eddie's closest pals at The Casino, a below street level pool hall downtown. He had also stopped by Jimmy's, a barbershop/pool hall housed in a rickety old building perched over the Susquehanna River in Wormleysburg practically under the Market Street Bridge. Graham had also been snooping around Top Dog, a favorite diner with outdoor tables, inside booths and a killer jukebox.

Eddie especially enjoyed taking Richard out for runs along

the creek and through the woods. On the last night there he and Neil dropped acid, and watched the Apollo moon walk on TV. Eddie wondered at the unreality of everything, yet he was completely in the moment. Neil was so high he couldn't speak, and laid down on a big Navajo rug with Richard.

    The next day Neil saw him to the gate at the D.C. airport and wished him the best. He stuffed some more cash into Eddie's pocket and said he looked forward to hearing from him. Eddie couldn't thank him enough. He had never been on a plane, was excited, and once airborne felt that he'd finally escaped. Nearly an hour into the flight the plane started experiencing turbulence that became severe. Eddie wasn't so sure he was safe after all. A sailor sitting across from him gripped his armrests, his eyes bulging as the jet bounced around in the unfriendly skies. Eddie was saying his last prayers too, but trying his best not to show it. After a few more panic stricken minutes the captain announced they were heading back, that an engine had gone out, but, that there was no need for concern. An hour later Eddie, already a veteran of the skies was fast asleep on another flight at 35,000 feet cruising over the center of the country.

***

    When Eddie rang the buzzer nobody answered. He rang again, was turning to leave when the door cracked open.

"Yes? What do you want?"

"Hi. Lindsey? Lindsey Brunner? Eddie Knox, one of Neil's students. He said he'd contacted you, and—"

"Oh, of course hon. Sorry. Come in."

    Lindsey was cute, around Neil's age and like him something of a hippie. She led Eddie up the stairway of the old Victorian into an apartment filled with plants, Indian pillows, abstract art, and stacks of art books on the floor.

"You don't mind sleeping in this room?" She pointed to an

ample couch covered with a comforter, a sheepskin, and Moroccan pillows.

"Perfect. Many thanks."

"Now, it's only for a week. That was the deal, then you'll stay with Rick and Sharon out by the beach. Agreed?"

"Agreed. If I can help any way around the apartment, dishes, housework, you name it."

"How sweet." She showed him a cabinet, and told him to unpack while she made him a sandwich. Eddie admired some healthy looking pot plants and pondered a grotesque painting of Jimi Hendrix that hung above the turntable.

The following day Eddie went out to explore the city. Downtown San Francisco was lively, and colorful. People were especially friendly, certainly not what he was used to back in the gray burg. He found himself flirting with two girls in Union Square park. The one he especially liked wrote down her number when her friend went into the St. Francis Hotel to use the restroom. Eddie told her how William Randolph Hearst railroaded Fatty Arbuckle, and ruined his career with lies about the death of a party goer there. Hearst, who by most accounts had a unhealthy God complex, had blamed Arbuckle and ignored the fact the girl was known "bad news" at parties. Looking over at the historic hotel Eddie was sure it had plenty more tales to tell.

When the girls left he walked to Chinatown. He was quickly enchanted, especially with the back alleys. He spent most of the day there before having a plate of chow mein on an outdoor terrace overlooking Portsmouth Square. He finished the day off back downtown catching the latest James Bond film. He had read all of the Bond books and they'd certainly inspired his own desire to one day write a thriller.

Lindsey was not there when he returned to the apartment. He was dying to get high. He wondered if he should take some off of her plants. On the coffee table he found a note that said: Enjoy this Eddie. And there was a fat joint. He put on an album he'd just bought by the 13th Floor Elevators and kicked back on the couch. Only a few songs in, Lindsey came through the door with a girl closer to his age. They smoked the rest of the joint together. They'd brought along albums by the Doors, Love, the Chamber Brothers and invited him to join them at a show at the Fillmore later. Eddie looked at the handout, saw that the headliner was The Everly Brothers. He said sure since he'd loved their songs when he was a kid. Lindsey said groovy, and her friend Gina produced some pungent Afghani hash and a pipe.

The allotted week flew by and next he moved out near the ocean in the deep Richmond District with Rick and Sharon. He had his own room, the guest room. The walls were lined with paperback books, and that pleased him. But Rick and Sharon were not exactly friendly and seemed distant. Eddie barely saw them during the stay. He found the cool, foggy area gloomsville and wondered if this was part of the reason why the couple appeared disgruntled. He did enjoy spooky Playland, the haunted appearing amusement strip above the crashing waves at Ocean Beach, and the crazed amplified laugh of Sal the fat lady. The ghostly aura influenced his journal writing. He spent some time wandering and hanging around there. He took long walks through Golden Gate Park, and rowed a rowboat out on a small man-made lake. His last night at Rick and Sharon's he listened to them screaming at each other half the night. From their paperback library he'd read *Steppenwolf, Catch-22*, and he left his own paperback *Stranger in a Strange Land* with them.

"Dusty" the next patron on Neil's list lived in North Beach, but he discovered from a neighbor she was on a motorcycle trip in Mexico. Eddie held his cardboard SANTA CRUZ sign at the freeway entrance and before long secured a ride the entire way. The driver was quite fat and talked about food most of the trip, going into great detail describing meals he'd prepared and eaten.

He spoke lovingly of their nuanced flavors, textures and consistencies. Eddie thought he would never stop talking about the variety and taste of various melons, his favorite fruit. Once in Santa Cruz Eddie walked around, and checked out the boardwalk. It reminded him somewhat of the Jersey shore. The beach was coaxing him and he peeled off his shirt, stretched out on a towel from his shoulder bag, and took a snooze in the morning sun. When he awoke a few hours later he knew right away he had one hell of a sunburn; he cursed himself for being so dumb.

The address that Neil had provided turned out to be a commune, a crumbling semi-mansion with a wide front porch cluttered with rattan furniture, a swing, piles of magazines, plants in buckets, and two sleeping dogs. On the surrounding property various tents, and hobo looking clapboard structures were thrown up, laundry hanging, piles of firewood. On the swing sat a hippie with a long beard wearing what looked like a monk's cloak and leaning on a walking staff. The hippie monk told him to go ahead inside, and get signed up. Inside Eddie found an office/living room of sorts with a jungle of plants; cats sleeping luxuriously on overstuffed velour furniture with stuffing sticking out in spots. A gray haired hippie woman at the desk told him to take the seat across from her. She asked for his ID. Eddie balked for a moment, told her he was looking for Mary Beaumont, who a friend said might be able to provide temporary board. The woman smiled. Eddie thought her eyes were like a Keene kid painting—tripping, no doubt.

"Sunshine, or rather Mary left only a week ago, back to New Orleans I understand. Someone gravely ill in her family. But, we can certainly put you up for two weeks, and then if you'd like to stay on we'll assign you a job. Sound fair?"

"Sounds great." Eddie handed over his ID although it gave him some pause. He figured a new ID was something he should look into once he was settled.

His bed was in a dormitory that was built onto the back of the house, reminding him of a barn. There were fifteen beds, but only a couple had personal belongings on them. He found his number near the end, and stashed his bag in a rack provided above. He was thinking he had to go out to buy some ointment for his back because the burn was starting to get to him. He wondered if he could even lie on it. Two pretty hippie girls came into the dorm. One asked if he was Eddie. They told him to get undressed and show them his burns. They pulled a special mat from out a closet and had him lie down. They proceeded to treat them with a cooling aloe vera/ mud pack. Eddie said it felt wonderful. He called them angels. They laughed and one kissed his ear.

 Later that evening there was a communal dinner under a tent fit for a circus. Bland yet filling vegetarian food was served. In one area Tarot cards were being read. Back massages were being given on some tables, acupuncture and ear candling on others. Some people were reading in overstuffed, beat up chairs. The heady smell of marijuana drifted in the air. In one area Eddie found two dudes who looked like members of The Byrds jamming. One had an acoustic guitar, the other a conga drum. Eddie sat across from them and one passed him a joint. After a few deep hits the duo started to sound pretty good to Eddie. The guitarist sang as well, sounding something like Neil Young. Life at the commune was sweet but ultimately boring for Eddie who still craved excitement.

 He dreamed of a significant crime pulled off smoothly, one where he would take in enough to live without financial worries for a long time. He wanted the right target though, some corporation for whom the robbery would ultimately mean little, with their insurance, obscene corporate wealth and all. At the commune he met no one who could possibly be a partner in such a crime, no, they were all too mellow with peace and love, and would be repulsed by the idea of crime. Eddie wasn't a hippie. He wore his hair in a shag like the British bands he liked. He dressed like a

Mod. In his earlier years he had dressed like a typical juvenile delinquent: leather jacket, pegged pants and pointy shoes. That had segued into a black semi-pimp look, then he'd done a 180 turn, switching to a Brooks Brothers collegiate look for a short period before going straight out Mod.

He did end up sleeping with the girl who had kissed his ear, who dressed in suede and fringes, and looked like a beautiful Indian squaw. On a lovely moonlit night they'd walked along the country road down to a beach. They smoked hashish in a kilim. They stayed there until dawn on blankets. For a moment Eddie considered staying on with his hippie squaw, but the idea of actually working at the place made him consider otherwise.

Eddie's SAN JOSE sign finally snagged him a ride after almost an hour. At first he was a little reluctant to get in since the man didn't look at him when he approached the passenger door. Eddie waited until he did, but it was quick. He was a big guy with choppy brown hair, a wig in fact and skin that looked like bread dough. Eddie was still a little on guard when he opened the door. "You going to San Jose?" In a kind of mocking voice the man answered a drawn out yeeees, and told him to get in. Eddie did, but was glad that he still carried his Buck knife strapped to his right boot. The driver said he could toss his bag into the back. Eddie said that was okay, straddling it with his legs. There was the after smell of consumed junk food. Eddie thought burger, and fries probably. There was a milkshake container in a holder with a bent straw and a take out bag between the driver's legs.

He pulled off onto the ramp, peeling out a bit. After a period of uncomfortable silence moving down the highway at a fair clip Eddie said he was going downtown. He asked how close he could get him to it. The driver ignored his question, and picked up speed. Eddie's right hand fell to his knife handle. The man puckered his lips like a fish. Eddie realized he was a freak and cursed himself for having accepted the ride.

"How'd ya like to make a little money sonny?"

"Uh, doing what?"

"Oh, nothing much, just joining me for a little relaxation time."

Eddie had his fist snug on the knife handle. He spoke in a voice he was trying to keep the fear out of: "Well, thank you sir, but no. People are expecting me."

"It wouldn't take long. Do you know what a traveler is? That's all I am. I wouldn't hurt you."

"Like I said no thanks, but I do appreciate the lift."

"Well, fuck you, then!" fish mouth said, all vicious. He pulled to the side of the highway in a screech kicking up gravel. "Get the fuck out then!" The mania in his face evaporated when he saw the Buck knife and the determined look on Eddie's face. He became all soft and squishy again, and smiled like a big stuffed animal.

"Listen sonny, please I-I didn't mean no harm, really. I'm just a poor soul looking for a little affection, and um, do have some trouble controlling my emotions. P-Please forgive me. We all have problems. Very sorry, really..."

"Downtown," was all that Eddie said, and when they arrived he re-sheathed his knife, climbed out without another word. He watched the car pull away. He hung out in a ragged park for a while calming himself, and then walked over to a diner to have a greasy breakfast. Afterward he began looking for the address Neil had provided. This one had no phone number either. It turned out to be a shit green house surrounded by a near dead yard, empty of any signs of life. He wondered if it was even occupied. He pressed the buzzer. A handsome man with a suspicious look wearing an open, brown leather aviator jacket and white T-shirt answered the door. Eddie introduced himself, explained his situation, and said that Neil had given him the address. The man's expression turned super friendly, and he invited him inside, patting him on the back.

In the living room there was a lot of beat up furniture, but nothing else, like a meeting room. Eddie would discover that's exactly what it was. The man's name was Zack; he was a college chum of Neil's. Once Eddie became comfortable they shared stories about Neil. Zack said that Eddie could crash as long as he liked, but would have to sleep on a couch. Eddie expressed his concerns with his ID because of the problems back in Pennsylvania. Zack waved it off, but said he would look into getting him California legal. Later, a couple others who lived there emerged sleepy from back bedrooms. They talked, sipped coffee, and listened to Eddie's adventures thus far.

Bill seemed to enjoy Eddie's tales the best. "Hey, Zack," he said, "let's bring him along today. He might enjoy it."

"Next time. He has ID issues I want to straighten out first."

"Wow, you're a wanted fugitive? I'm impressed," said Bill.

His girlfriend Cathy, who was leaning on him, smiled weakly.

Eddie said he'd mostly been unlucky to get caught up in the juvenile probation system, stemming from truancy and running away from home. He failed to mention that he'd been involved in a number of robberies and car thefts. But, he reasoned, he'd never been caught for any of those acts, so why bring them up? Eddie was to learn that Zack, Bill and the others were left wing activists, currently demonstrating for Caesar Chavez. Eddie listened to them talk about the action, and the excitement at the last demonstration. Some had been arrested, and some targeted by the police, they claimed. Eddie could see their enthusiasm and passion for their cause. Like the hippie philosophy of peace and love, the political spectrum didn't interest Eddie much either, but these new providers made it all sound cool.

Eddie was pleased when joints were lit. The pot was especially strong. Someone switched on FM radio, and everyone grooved out to "Green Onions" by Booker T and the MGs. Eddie came to be looked on as a kind of mascot by the others. They took turns trying to teach him about politics. What they were saying made some sense to Eddie. He had no doubt that the government was corrupt to the gills. He had been through the juvenile probation and court system. Most teachers, parents, employers were to him a microcosm or mirror of the government: repressive, criminal, and against freedom in one way or another. On the other hand he felt some kind of basic government was needed to protect citizens against real crimes and enemies. He understood why they called the cops pigs immediately though. He'd had some first hand experience with that.

When Bill began schooling him on the illegal Vietnam war he became more interested since he'd barely escaped being drafted himself. He had one friend who had joined the Coast Guard when he became 1A, and two other friends who'd taken off for Canada. Eddie was thinking of heading to Canada as well before he was busted for an ounce of weed. That time he'd finally landed in the regular adult section of Dauphin Country Prison. He had only been in the small juvenile section before for probation violations. Bill was impressed with his jail experiences even though Eddie's time spent behind bars only amounted to a few months. The pot bust had earned him a step up in the system to "special probation" and was explained to him as being more akin to parole. The pal he was busted with, whose name was on the apartment lease was offered a deal: enlist or go to reform school. He enlisted. Eddie was not given that choice, but instead placed on three years special probation.

Bill talked enthusiastically about a group called the Weathermen; he knew someone closely involved. They sounded like bad asses willing to take drastic action against the war. Bill loaned Eddie books by angry Black Panthers, the heady Timothy Leary, chapbooks on anarchy, and filled his head with romantic freedom fighter adventures suggesting that this may be his path as well. Zack meanwhile worked with him on obtaining California ID legitimately as their hippie lawyer advised. Eddie passed the driver's test and before long had a legit California drivers license. He cut up his old Pennsylvania ID.

"We checked," said Zach. "You're not considered a fugitive, so this is gold, my man. You didn't commit any violence or robberies so your case will be an insignificant item."

As friendly and helpful as they had all been, two weeks later Eddie decided to move on. The activist scene, although he was sympathetic, was in the end not for him. They wished him well and arranged a ride to take him to San Francisco where he could take a bus over to Berkeley to check out the last patron that Neil had most generously provided. He called Neil from the "headquarters" as they referred to Zack's decrepit, moldy house. Neil was pleased to hear from him. He said there had been no new inquiries about him, so they had surely written him off.

"But, had you stayed here you'd definitely have been locked up, probably for a year or more. I spoke with Mr. Patterson and he was certain of that."

Eddie thanked him and promised to stay in touch. Eddie called "Laura" his next provider, in Berkeley but there was no answer.

Eddie found San Francisco's morning fog and its cool as an air-conditioner weather a downer after the summery South Bay. He was glad to be continuing on his way. He boarded the bus for Berkeley. The college town was quite different with an almost village-like atmosphere. The streets were lined with quaint little ramshackle houses and clumps of trees and flora. The place was populated with hippies and many students attending the famous university. Eddie wandered up and down Telegraph Avenue and had a sandwich with a bunch of sprouts sticking out of it that he wasn't too sure about, but found were edible. He had a strong cup of coffee at a popular hangout/coffee house, and called Laura from a pay phone. A bulletin board, covered with tacked up messages, bore advertisements for: roommates wanted, rides to Big Sur offered, jobs, garage sales, astral readings, meditation, yoga teachers and so on.

Laura answered right away, and said sure he could stay as long as he liked. She needed a new roommate since hers had just split, and could he pay half the rent?

Even as frugal as he had been, with the free rooms and many free meals, Eddie's money was dwindling. But he had enough for half of the month's rent and agreed. She gave him directions. Her place was only a few blocks away.

The apartment was in the back of an unpainted wooden building on the second floor, overlooking a backyard overgrown with weeds, and plants. A bench squatted under a kumquat tree, beside a small vegetable garden. The porch outside her door was crowded with potted plants and a collapsing wicker chair. She must have heard him coming up the steps since she stepped out from behind the screen door. She gave him a big smile: freckles, tied back thick, red tresses, barefoot. She smelled of flowers and an immediate big sister relationship was born. They hit it off famously and right away as people sometimes do on first meetings.

After some story sharing, red wine, and a meal of pasta/salad Eddie offered a joint from a lid of Acapulco Gold he'd purchased through Bill back at the Headquarters. Laura laughed, said she hadn't smoked mary jane in a long while. A few hits changed her mood completely. She became animated, and lively. She kissed Eddie on the forehead like a big sister, put on a Beatles album, and began to dance and sing along. Eddie had never seen anyone react to pot in this way and found it amusing. Laura, he learned, was a nurse, and was gone all day. When she came home she would take a long bath, eat a huge salad, and go off to a coffee shop with friends, usually returning after he was asleep.

Eddie explored the town during the day, haphazardly looking

for work. He was a bit taken aback when a record store owner took a liking to his Mod clothes, his knowledge of British Invasion, blues, rhythm and blues, and early rock 'n roll, and offered him a part time job. Eddie took it, but when he found that his paycheck would barely pay for the records he'd put aside, he decided that this was not the job for him.

And he still dreamed of that big heist. After more than two months, he hadn't committed any crimes, and only thought about doing so when he checked his dwindling money supply.

He next took a job as a telephone solicitor, and found that he was better than good. The first week he took home nearly four hundred dollars. The other seasoned solicitors looked at him in awe. Who this wunderkind, they wondered, was who had strolled in off the street and scored like that.

He sold ads in a newspaper with a dubious (from what Eddie could see) connection to the police department. The masthead was an equally dubious looking badge. Salesmen could call off a coveted repeat ad buyer's list handed out by the manager like some holy oracle, or call cold names from the phone book. Newcomers were given the phone book, so Eddie's performance was doubly impressive. When he was given the repeat list his sales went through the roof. Soon he was looked upon as a kind of god of the boiler room. They nicknamed him The Young Horn God, the horn being boiler speak for the phone.

Eddie didn't know why he was so good, but as soon as he heard the voice on the other end, some instinct told him what kind of tone and attitude to take. He was rarely wrong, but even if he was, he could still often save it and end up closing the sale. His trick was to convince himself that he was doing something good, worthwhile, and only suggesting the person at the other end do the same. An almost other mind clicked in, another intelligence, and captured the sucker. Yes — *sucker*. Eddie knew that one was born every minute. It was the same inner voice reminding him of

the spectacular robbery he would one day pull off.
Eddie became friendly with Mark, another hot shot solicitor, and his only real competition. They competed in good spirits, and made it fun. The winner of the day had to buy dinner, and drinks after work. It was a fairly even give and take. They shared an interest in music too; some evenings they visited the numerous beer soaked bars that featured authentic blues artists. They knew the bands they liked, the Stones, the Kinks, the Pretty Things, and so on, were influenced by U.S. blues, and here they had an opportunity to see a lot of them in a number of intimate bars and clubs that populated the city at that time. John Lee Hooker, The Paul Butterfield Blues Band, Sonny Terry and Brownie Mcgee, Juke Boy Bonner, Charlie Musselwhite (who Eddie saw mowing his lawn one day and who had a pay phone installed on his front porch), Junior Wells, Buddy Guy, Lowell Folsom and many more played regular gigs and they saw them all. At a Hooker show they watched the feeling-no-pain blues godfather fall off of his stool, get back up, take another drink and continue on. "Boom Boom Boom" indeed.

Eddie had not completely forgotten about his writing skill and Neil's advice. But he'd only written one story. One weekend, when he'd been too high on coke for his own good, he'd barely slept or ate, and stayed up all night, filling spiral notebook after spiral notebook with a science fiction story he concocted from notes he'd made one day coming down from from a trip and looking over a revolving rack of sci fi paperbacks in a bookstore. He used notes regarding the different covers as prompters for his story. Once he recovered from the night of coke and writing, had some sleep (taking a sick day at work), ate a decent breakfast, and, reread his story in the light of day, he was dismayed at how awful it was. He ripped it up and tossed it in the trash. He decided then and there that he needed more experience before attempting to write anything else. He decided that cocaine was not a good writing drug, and was not for him.

Eddie decided to walk up Telegraph through the campus, meander his way through, and over to the other side, visit the record store he'd worked at briefly, Rather Ripped Records. As he approached the campus, a crowd blocked the way, spreading out, shouting. The mob was moving toward him.

Students held signs: END THE WAR! OUT OF VIETNAM! People were ran past him. "The pigs are coming! Run!"

Eddie turned down a side street but it too was packed with confused and angry demonstrators, running willy-nilly in every direction. One guy held his bleeding head, long hair matted with blood. Terror contorted his face. The roar of the crowd and the incoherent police bullhorns only added to the chaos.

Eddie ran with a group of protesters. He smelled the tear gas before he felt the sting in his eyes. He looked back, saw a unit of riot geared police with clubs coming on fast in pursuit of his group. Around one corner Eddie broke from the crowd and ducked into a doorway of a building to hide. He watched the pigs storm by. He stayed hidden as his heartbeat gradually slowed. It was a while before he felt it was safe to come out.

***

One morning Eddie found Laura still at home. She was making pancakes, coffee. Two fruit salads awaited on the table. She was taking a few vacation days (or she would lose them). She planned on enjoying herself. She wanted to take Eddie out to dinner at a friend's newly opened restaurant that night. It was interesting seeing her eat something besides salads, Eddie thought, but he wasn't much for breakfast since he ran on caffeine, and didn't get hungry till around noon.

He told her about the demonstration and his near escape. She told him that she and a girlfriend were walking through campus the night before and a tall, skinny, black man leapt out of some bushes stark naked, scaring them half to death, and then pranced off like a deer. She laughed about it, but said at the time he had really scared them. Another friend told her he was a campus oddball known as "The Prancing Ghost."

A scratching at the screen door heralded the arrival of Bruno the squirrel, looking for a handout. Laura had somehow trained him to eat out of her hand. She went to it with a snack, spoke to it, even stroked it. To please Laura, Eddie did the best he could with the breakfast, finished dressing, and rushed off to work.

At the tele-marketing offices, the door was padlocked. A wordy city notice was tacked to the door. Another sticker in red letters stated the business was closed by the IRS. Eddie found Mark sitting in the stairway, smoking a cigarette.

"Yeah, we're fucked," he said. "I called old man Garrison and the poor guy was actually crying. He's leaving for Lodi. It's all over Eddie. I hope you saved."

Eddie had saved. He would be good for a while, but just when he had found a niche it was gone. He didn't want to spend his life as a phone solicitor, but for the foreseeable future he had planned on raking in some dough and, like Bruno the squirrel, stashing it away before making his next move.

Now it was back to square one.

He went with Mark to his apartment. They dimmed the lights, smoked some dope, sipped Sangria, and listened to "Let It Bleed." Later, while wearing shades, and satisfying their munches at a fast food joint Mark became optimistic.

"Listen Eddie I have an idea to make some real loot. Are you interested?"

"Sure."

Eddie had talked about his idea of pulling off a robbery since they had become closer friends, and had explained his criteria for such a crime. Mark had laughed, so Eddie figured he had not taken him seriously, but now Mark said in a lower voice:

"I know a place we can hit, and it's easy and should be a nice haul."

Mark's previous job was at a swanky restaurant on the marina that did a fantastic business. The cash he claimed was locked up overnight in the manager's office, and that there was no safe. By accident he had seen the boss stuffing the cash bag at night's end into a wooden desk drawer.

"How do you know that's still the way it's done?"

"The boss is a lazy fuck, and a cheap stiff," Mark confided. "I'm betting things haven't changed."

"How do we get in? Alarms? Is there a guard or watchman?"

"No, Eddie, none of that. There's a notice in the front window that says that the place has a security system, but it's bogus. I overheard the boss joking with someone on the phone about it once, that it was a phony sign. The boss thought that was hilarious. Like I said, a cheap-ass fucker. We get in because I have a key to the back entrance. We'd have to break into his office, and break open the drawer probably, but that's it."

"And the take?"

"We hit it on a Sunday night after the weekend haul, and before the cash would go to the bank Monday morning. I'm thinking twenty grand, maybe more. I've watched the waitresses ringing up the bills, lots of moolah my friend, let me tell you."

"The cops would go back and interview everyone who'd worked there."

"I doubt that, and besides I plan on moving to Hawaii right afterwards."

Eddie's heist fantasy always featured a bigger take — maybe a hundred grand, or at *least* fifty grand — but here was an opportunity to get back into the game with a partner and up his cash holdings significantly. Was it worth the risk of prison? He couldn't quite decide. He didn't want to appear chicken to his friend whom he had bragged to and exaggerated his criminal exploits.

"When did you want to do it?"

"Whenever you say."

Eddie told Mark he wanted to check the place out, go by for either lunch or dinner, and take a look after hours. He was thinking he could take Laura there as a treat, since she was taking him someplace. He left Mark with a head full of ideas on the score. It was exciting. He felt his criminal mindset being reborn, that thirst for getting something else by illegal means blossoming. His persona itself seemed to change since he had a new purpose. A Stones tune that seemed to mirror his train of thought and emotion came to him. He sang some of the lyrics out loud as he strolled down Telegraph Avenue.

"You can't always get what you want
But if you try sometimes you might find
You get what you need
Oh yeah..."

Dinner with Laura was at her friend's house that she had turned into a restaurant. The house was chopped up into small rooms filled with tables and chairs. Eddie felt it strange that she also lived there. The food was good down-home cooking. It was a pleasant evening with too much wine. Because of that Eddie turned in early. Laura stayed up with her boyfriend who'd been waiting on the steps when they returned. Eddie had known nothing about him before. He was an intern who Eddie found off-putting, condescending. He wore a nearly constant smirk and asked nosey questions. Eddie hoped this was not the face or personality of the new generation of doctors. Laura didn't seem aware of any of this, and was under his spell.

Later he heard them balling, but it sounded short lived. When Eddie used the bathroom he heard the loud snoring of Dr. Quickie and found Laura in the kitchen digging into a carton of ice cream. She didn't see him, so he quietly went back to bed.

Dinner at the snazzy Waterfront Pier Restaurant was memorable. Eddie's reservations were under a false name. They were given a small window table with a view of the bay and a fishing pier. Laura was excited, having known about the place, but never having been there. Eddie told her he'd received a substantial bonus and wanted to celebrate when she expressed concern over the price. As far as Laura knew he was still working. The wooded parking lot was surrounded by trees leaning in one direction, and other vegetation around the edges of the water. The setting sun gave the scene the soft glow of an Impressionist painting. On arrival Eddie scanned the main room, and looked over the well-heeled clientele. On a trip to the restroom he tried looking into the office marked "Manager" that Mark had told him about, but found it locked. Later he used the john again, and this time it was open. He looked in, and didn't see any safe. Just a partially eaten meal, a twisted napkin, and a half-empty glass of red wine.

Laura was especially enjoying herself, and complimented Eddie to the point he finally told her to stop. If she continued it would ruin the evening. Her big doe eyes said that she understood; she touched his arm.

"Sorry," she said, "you're right. Let's enjoy ourselves."

From that point on they did just that having second cocktails, appetizers, followed by juicy steaks, string beans with slivers of almonds, garlicky mashed potatoes, and a bottle of Pinot Noir from the Napa Valley. Over coffee and a fat piece of chocolate truffle cake they shared Laura broke the disappointing news that she was transferring to San Diego in one month.

Eddie moved in with Mark to save on rent. They planned the robbery after Eddie made a few more visits to the restaurant at different hours. They secured the proper tools for breaking into the office door, and desk drawer. They bought dark hooded sweatshirts, crazy-looking Zorro masks, special gloves from a gun shop, and a backpack for the score money.

Finally, the target night arrived.

2

The inner restaurant looked dark except for a couple of dull night lights. Eddie was in a hyperaware state. He could hear the sound of vehicles whooshing by in the outer layers of his consciousness: night sounds, electric sounds, everything exaggerated now. They removed their masks. Mark looked a bit nervous and against Eddie's instructions had imbibed more than a few belts of vodka. Eddie was looking at his shit smile in the near dark, wondering if he was the best partner after all. Mark slid the key in, turned it, and like the night they had pre-tested, no alarm went off. They stepped into the back hallway. They stopped and listened for a couple of minutes. They made their way to the office door, found it unlocked, but Eddie was suspicious.

"Maybe someone is still inside."

Mark's scrunched expression said he didn't think so; he started to go for the desk, but Eddie stopped him.

"Wait goddamnit," he hissed, and sure enough they heard someone walking inside the building, walking heavily, too. A flashlight coming from the adjoining hallway made Eddie close the door quietly. They ducked behind the desk. The door was opened and a flashlight swept the room once. The light disappeared as the door shut once more again.

They waited what seemed a long time, and then heard a door being shut somewhere, more walking, talking, two voices, and then quiet, real quiet for a good long spell. They listened and it remained quiet. Eddie told Mark to stay put. Out in the foyer he peered over the window sill by a slight space the curtain failed to cover. There was a car idling out front with two people in it. It pulled off. He sat there a while longer until he was sure they were indeed alone. Still he crept back to the room, turned on the light.

"Okay, which drawer?"

Mark emerged still showing some fear in his eyes. He seemed to be having trouble expressing himself, but managed to point to the deep bottom drawer. It was locked. Eddie pried it open with a crowbar, breaking the wood, making a loud noise. Eddie was thrilled because there it was: a canvas money bag, and by the looks of it, stuffed. He looked inside and saw a lot of green.

"We got it! Let's get the fuck out of here!"

He packed the bag into the knapsack, strapped it on. Mark was laughing. "See I told you fucker." They let themselves out the back way, hoods up, masks on and only removed them once they traversed all of Seawall Drive, and had passed not one vehicle.

$42,448.00 was spread out on the glass coffee table. Eddie and Mark stared at it, took turns hitting a joint, exclaiming: Fuck yeah! Far fucking out! Eddie broke his vow, did a couple bumps of Mark's blow. They sipped brandy.

"Far fucking out!" Mark kept saying walking around the money viewing it from different angles. Once the jubilation had died down they became serious again, divided the funds, and a certain level of paranoia set in. A "it's too good to be true" feeling settled over them and neither ended up sleeping much. The next day they had the thrill of reading about the robbery in the paper: "an undisclosed amount was stolen."

Three days later Mark departed on a flight to Honolulu. He gave Eddie the name of a place he liked to hang out there: a way to get in touch if he should ever decide to visit. Mark sang all of the island's praises, but when Eddie considered Hawaii he always thought of his crazy old mother taking hula lessons at the Y in the cold Pennsylvania winter months. The wacky island music coming from the bedroom where she practiced. Mark made it sound interesting, describing its perfect beaches, warm surfing waters, and throngs of pretty girls. Once Mark was gone Eddie would become an avid viewer of the TV series *Hawaii Five O*, and indeed develop a yearning to one day visit the archipelago.

Mark left him with a so-so one bedroom apartment, a battered stereo, a coffee percolator, dishes, silverware and some books by Carlos Castaneda that Mark had never cracked. Eddie did, and they led to more esoteric thinking. During his second year in Berkeley and once an intense affair with a coed ended badly Eddie wondered why he was still there. He had found being dumped by the preppie vixen more heart-breaking than he was prepared for. Eddie hadn't cried like that since he was a kid. The coed went back to her football star boyfriend. She had brilliantly used Eddie as the jealousy factor. He weathered the breakup by immersing himself into his music, most of which the coed hated, especially Black Sabbath's "Paranoid". He played that one over and over, as loud as he could get away with in the daytime, and with headphones at night. He did some part-time phone solicitor work for another outfit that was more regulated, and not nearly as lucrative. He decided to move across the bay to San Francisco.

He looked at a few seedy places in the Polk Gulch area, better ones on lower Nob Hill, but there was something he didn't like about them all: noise (bad rock music from above), no view, low ceilings, an off smell in the hallway, funky bathroom, a crying baby next door. He was considering heading out to the Richmond District, or to the Haight to look at more when a yen for chow mein directed him to take a bus to Chinatown. The waitress, a cute Chinese girl took a liking to him. They flirted since business was slow, and her boss didn't seem to mind. When she heard of his quest she said that she might know of something, and told him to wait. He sipped jasmine tea, looked out the window at an old woman with the common bowl-cut hairstyle wearing loose black shirt and pants, pushing a cart stacked with crates full of live chickens. A feeble Chinese man followed pulling a cardboard box of bok choy by a rope. Linlang came back with a big smile and handed him a piece of paper.

"Our friend the doctor has a small place for rent right here, well, nearby. Go now. He is expecting you." Eddie thanked her, even kissed her hand which made her look a little embarrassed. Off he went following her hand drawn map. Chinatown, already enchanting to Eddie now took on a glow of an illuminated film coming to life. The place seemed to pulse with mystery and energy. He savored the smell of the joss sticks. He was wowed by the gaudy Buddha stores blasting gold and red from their inner-shops into darkened alleyways like a visual bomb. He passed a club, and heard the clattering sounds of mahjong tiles being shuffled. An ancient Chinese man sat on a tall stool at the entranceway eating dark noodles out of a lacquered container with flashing chopsticks. Eddie bought some healthy looking black plums from an outdoor fruit stand. He found the doctor's address in one of Chinatown's alleyways, above a board painted red along with some indented black Chinese characters. He rang the buzzer by the grimy gated door that read: D.Kublar. The door was opened by a Chinese dwarf wearing black silk pajamas and a matching cap. A long pigtail hung down his back. He smiled like a cat. Eddie introduced himself, said that he was inquiring about the apartment. "Ah so," the dwarf bowed slightly. "Follow prease." Eddie followed him up a staircase that led to the next floor where he continued to the end of the hall, then up a narrow spiral stairway. He warned Eddie to watch his step.

At the top floor Eddie stepped into an opulent room full of black lacquer furniture, dimmed lights, Chinese tapestry screens, gaudy vases, figurines, exotic plants and such. The dwarf gestured to a seat, asked if he would like tea. On his second cup another presence entered the room, a tall, thin man dressed in a flamboyant purple and golden cloak. Eddie stood. The man was bald but had a Fu Manchu beard. The oddest thing was that Eddie felt he looked more Caucasian than Oriental. He introduced himself as Dr. Kublar, shook Eddie's hand, and pleasantly asked him to be seated. Eddie couldn't help but notice the many rings he wore, a couple of them flashed when he gestured. He spoke Chinese to the dwarf who he called Mu. Dr. Kublar sat across from Eddie in an extravagant chair and folded his arms. In the dull light Eddie looked at his possible new landlord, and indeed detected some Oriental linage around the eyes. Dr. Kublar said: "Edward, may I call you Edward?"

Eddie remembered the only one who had ever called him that, a benevolent uncle. The uncle was a confirmed bachelor, well traveled, and smoked expensive cigars. He had let Eddie stay at his swanky apartment on one of his attempts to runaway from home. The uncle worked as a liaison with his parents, and eventually negotiated a return sans punishment. But, when Eddie ran away again, later that year he refused to let him stay, although he did give him some money, which made sense since he was an ex-banker. The uncle was tall and thin like Dr. Kublar. They even shared a similar quick smile.

"Edward, I recently arrived here from Tibet. I inherited this building. On the level below is a small apartment that I have no use for, this floor is more than adequate for myself and Mu. Lo fan, that is you, Caucasian or white ghost..." he said, laughed. "... are rarely rented to here, although as you see I too have much white blood, yet, you see how I dress and look?"

"I see the Oriental in your eyes."

"I have Tibetan blood, but I'm mostly of Swiss stock. It's a long story. In fact a story I'm putting to paper now, my memoirs if you will. Mu is my transcriber. I have lived a life that is almost unbelievable, well, in fact is unbelievable, yet all very true."

Eddie sipped tea and watched Dr. Kublar snuggle a holder onto a blue cigarette and then light it. The light from the flame in the semi-dark room made his face appear mystical, even diabolical at times. Eddie felt like he'd stepped into one of the supernatural tales he liked to read.

"Now, please Edward, tell me about yourself, and how you ended up here looking for an apartment."

Eddie began. There was something about this man that demanded honesty. He almost felt like he was back in a confessional, although there he had never told the priests everything. He had always been suspect of authority, but Dr. Kublar was different. He felt that here was a special individual, someone who had wisdom and projected an almost unworldly energy. Eddie thought having an apartment here would be fantastic. He told him everything, except about certain previous crimes, especially the last heist. Dr. Kublar asked if he had any prospects of a job lined up. Eddie admitted that he didn't, but he had enough money saved to last the rest of the year, if the rent wasn't too steep.

"Edward, I like you, but you are not without some problems. I have the ability to read people quite well, and although I feel you have a good soul, there is a troublesome area in your psyche that needs to be resolved, and for that reason I will offer you the apartment. I'd like to work with you on some of these matters. I believe everything happens for a reason. As my tenant I offer you an open invitation to come and talk whenever you'd like. You can talk to me about anything, unlike those charlatan priests of your earlier years."

Eddie hadn't mentioned priests, he'd only had a passing thought about the confessional experience. Eddie wondered what exactly Dr. Kublar was suggesting. He wondered what the apartment to let was like. As if reading that thought Dr. Kublar clapped his hands, Mu reentered the room, silent and expressionless.

"Please show Mr. Knox the room Mu, and then we'll continue our conversation."

It was a studio apartment, but it was charming, picturesque if you will, with a window view in the kitchenette that looked over rooftops at the top half of a pagoda. Eddie felt for a moment that he had been transported to somewhere in Asia, even to another time. The main room held a single bed, a dresser with a cloudy mirror, dark hardwood floors, small Oriental table, a wooden chair, a night stand, a lamp shaped like a lotus. Eddie would have to make the bed into more of a sitting couch in the daytime. It being up against a wall that could easily be done with the right cover, some pillows. The bathroom was impeccably clean, a small bathtub that Eddie could never fit into, but with a shower, so not a problem. What he really loved was that it was amazingly quiet, at least at the moment. He asked Mu if it was always this quiet. "Vely quiet Mr. Edward. Vely quiet."

The rent was so low that Eddie felt a bit guilty getting out his checkbook to pay Dr. Kublar for the first, the last month, and a deposit. He had opened a bank account with some of his loot, perfect for these kind of payments, but the doctor shook his finger in the air: "I prefer cash if you don't mind Edward."

Dr. Kublar looked at a note that Mu handed him. He sighed and explained to Eddie that they would have to continue their conversation later, that something had come up that he had to attend to.

"Mu will give you the keys. We'll catch up once you've settled in."

Edward stood and handed Dr. Kublar the paper bag of plums. The doctor looked inside and smiled.

"Thank you. You are most kind Edward. These will be perfect for my meeting."

Dr. Kublar took one out and handed it to Mu who looked at

it, sniffed it, said:

"Vely good. Vely sweet."

On the bus ride back to Berkeley Eddie marveled at the day, and the serendipity of finding such a cheap, out of sight apartment in Chinatown. He looked at his face and hands reflected in the window. He seemed to be moving in some spirit world, but the body odor of a fat hippie sitting across the aisle brought him back to reality. He moved closer to the back the bus, opened a window. The next day he rented a car, and over the next couple days moved into the new place. He began to arrange the apartment to suit him. At an antique store in Berkeley he bought a curious old sea chest. The clerk showed him the false bottom for keeping money or valuables. He would never had guessed it was there, the workmanship was so fine. The curmudgeon owner however would not barter so Eddie paid a high price, but he could afford it, and it was exactly what he needed. In his new place he transferred heist cash from his travel bag into the false bottom, it seemed tailor made for it. He filled the rest of the chest with sweaters, a few shirts, and once closed, he placed an Indian prayer mat, and a small pillow on top. In a drawer, in a cigar box he kept some spending cash that a thief would likely find, grab and leave with Eddie reasoned, but the place felt quite secure to him anyway.

Eddie decided to buy some new clothes, his Mod gear that had been mostly purchased in Philadelphia, and New York was showing real signs of wear. He had found that a certain style of ladies fitted jackets from the fifties and sixties were similar to the Mod jacket, so he refreshed his gear with a few he'd found in Berkeley thrift stores. In the Haight was a shop that carried real English gear, and some US copies. He bought new shirts, a belt, a gray vest, a pair of black wool tapered slacks, a scarf, a velour jacket and a fitted double breasted overcoat for a winter that was quickly approaching. He treated himself to a haircut too, since his shag had grown out and was looking tired.

He walked around the Haight imagining what it had been like in its heyday. There were still some peace and love types around, barefoot with flowers in their hair, and saucer eyes, smelling of patchouli oil. But another element was visible too: characters who looked to Eddie like exploiters. He spotted two dudes in ratty leather jackets selling dope out of the trunk of a car. He ended up scoring a lid from an older hippie chick who was their look out. She told him they mostly sold speed. He wasn't interested. At a trippy looking two level coffee shop he relaxed with his purchases. As he stirred his herbal tea, he saw someone he knew from Harrisburg coming in through the front door. Eddie didn't really know the guy: "Richmond" but they knew some of the same people, and knew each other by sight. Eddie had heard that Richmond had worked as a male hustler, with a couple of sugar daddies back in the burg. One of Eddie's friends told him that Richmond wasn't homosexual though. Richmond was infamous for carrying a sword cane, but he didn't have with him now. Maybe he carried a blade though like me, Eddie thought.

"Hey! Eddie, right? When did you get here?"

"Richmond?" They shook hands and Richmond took the chair across from him. Eddie said, "Oh, I've been here a while now, but I traveled around the Bay Area at first, then I settled over in Berkeley, but I live here now."

"Berkeley is far out, I hear. I need to get over there for a look see." The coffee shop was trying to hold onto the feeling of the dying hippie era. Walls were painted in various pastel swirls, and flowers in vases were set here and there. A cheerful vibe permeated the place: two levels of tables, booths, lots of tall plants, with some low sitar rock in the background and artwork that reminded Eddie of some of his better acid trips.

"If those poor suckers back in the burg could see us now eh?" Richmond said, looking outside where two buskers had set up. As they launched into a number, a beautiful hippie girl started dancing in a circle, laughing, looking pretty stoned. She fell on her ass, but got back up, smiled, and went back into her romp.

Richmond had grown his hair long, cut evenly at the shoulders and had beginnings of a spit curl mustache. He wore a tweedy suit, a jacket with epaulets, and a string tie. He was like a character from Mark Twain's era Eddie thought.

"Do you live over here?" Eddie asked as Richmond took a snort of snuff from a little wooden box. He offered it to Eddie who said no thanks.

"Just around the corner. I arrived here two weeks ago, but I lived here the summer of '66, too. The place is not what it used to be Eddie, but it's something like the Village, eh?"

"Yes, something like it." Eddie remembered New York, the first time, on a weekend to buy drugs to sell back in the burg. The introduction to the connection in the Village had been arranged by none other than Richmond. Eddie remembered his friend Herbert had grumbled about having to pay Richmond a finder's fee, but Eddie felt it was well worth it. He found the Village a fascinating place and thought he might eventually move there. They had bought a bunch of acid and grass from a flamboyant dealer who as Eddie remembered had six different types of locks on his door and had painted his Bass Weejuns lime green. They had taken the Greyhound back to the burg and made some good money on the exchange.

A couple weeks later they went back to New York to score again. That time they'd hitchhiked to save money. They were picked up right away, but were dumped by a freeway exit outside of Newark. They had just stuck out their thumbs again, when a police car pulled over. The cops asked them if they had heard about the riots. They hadn't, and the cops laughed. They copied down their ID information, told them they were doing that in case they turned up dead later. Eddie remembered looking at the city again, seeing black smoke billowing up at different points. The cops pulled off, and they remained nervous until they managed to score another ride.

"Do you wanna trip?" Richmond asked, opening a small, round pill container with a Hindu dancer on the lid. He took out a tab, put it on his own tongue. He picked another out, looked at Eddie expectantly. Eddie opened his mouth and Richmond placed it on his tongue. They talked some more, about people they both knew, what had become of them, not much by either account. Eddie was sorry to hear that a couple of his friends had been arrested for drugs. Richmond said that the burg cops were on the warpath against all freaks, which was what heads, hippies, rock musicians, old beatniks, bikers and assorted eccentric artists were called there. Richmond told him the bad news that "The Zoo" a communal apartment near the river that was a safe haven had been raided and closed down. Eddie had spent a couple of fun weeks there once when he had run away.

Richmond's face began seriously melting and Eddie said: "Oh wow man, I'm starting to get off."

"Right on. Let's go to my place. It's much groovier." Richmond helped Eddie with his packages.

Eddie marveled that his arms and legs were elongating as he walked. He became downright giddy. He said "out of sight" more than a couple times. Once inside the old Victorian he was having definite trouble maneuvering. Richmond guided him into a dim, comfy looking living room. Eddie fell into an overstuffed chair. He closed his eyes and watched an entirely new universe appear with different laws of physics in play: a kaleidoscope of new terrain, one where creatures spoke to him telepathically, floated upside down, and one eyed fish men tended a tall, willowy sea garden. A couple hours later when Eddie was stable, and able to function, he hit the hash pipe Richmond offered. Richmond was smiling like the Mad Hatter, actually wearing a stovepipe hat, and saying: "Primo fuckin' acid huh?"

"Yes, fantastic."

"Pure Owsley. Do you want to buy some?"

"Sure, sure."

Richmond's friend Matt came into the room with an acoustic guitar. He took a stool across the room, and began strumming, singing a tune he'd just written. Eddie was impressed. He was reminded of Mick Jagger or Jim Morrison. Richmond was a drummer, and said that he and Matt were forming a group. Eddie wished he played an instrument.

In that curious state after tripping Eddie waited for the bus watching a group of Hare Krishnas chanting, playing drums, burning incense, and asking pedestrians for donations. Eddie found the chant hypnotizing, and still savoring some psychedelic residue from the trip, almost missed the bus. Now Eddie had a steady connection for pot, acid, magic mushrooms, even coke although he really didn't care for that drug. The others at Richmond's place seemed cool, although they all complained too that the Haight was over and dead, that it was time to move on.

"Too bad you didn't make it out here three years ago baby," one chubby girl wearing multiple Indian bead necklaces, and kohl accentuated eyes told him while rolling a fat joint. "Golden Gate Park transformed itself into Eden there for a while."

Later, when Eddie entered Chinatown and approached his place in the alley he felt that he already lived in an entirely different world. The door opened before he could insert his key. Out filed three bald monks wearing light gray cloaks. They had yellow dots painted on their shaved heads. They were slightly bowed, wore glasses, and had their hands held together behind them. Inside the smell of incense was strong. The striking of a gong three times came from Dr. Kublar's apartment. Eddie slept soundly, deeply. He awoke to a light tapping on his door, saw dawn light leaking in from a space in the flimsy curtains that he reminded himself again he needed to change.

"Yes, who is it?" Eddie said with some agitation in his voice.

"Mr. Edward, so solly. The doctor wishes to speaky with you. Velly important."

"Right now?"

"Prease come up when you ready. Thank you."

Eddie grumbled, sat up wishing he could sleep a while longer. He put a light on, and went into the tiny bathroom. His pupils were still large. His rough tongue and mouth tasted vaguely chemical. He ran some water into the basin, stuck his head under it once it had warmed. He brushed his teeth, combed his hair and put on the new red and blue striped bathrobe he'd purchased downtown (at a ridiculous high price) over his also pricey dark blue pajamas. Eddie was torn over the money from the heist. Part of him wanted to spend like crazy, but he knew that was dumb. A smarter part of him wanted to keep it low key, make it last. He stepped into gray suede, monogrammed bedroom slippers that were also purchased on that shopping spree.

He had been in a devil-may-care buying mood that day. He splurged on an absurdly expensive dinner at a five star restaurant. He saw an attractive, well dressed Mod couple eating from a window seat. "I can eat here, too," he thought — but he found the food overly rich and overly done, the waiter smug and condescending, so, for his bill that was the better part of fifty dollars he left the waiter a one dollar tip. He had a good laugh when he left, and that helped rationalize blowing so much money.

He locked his door and climbed up to Dr. Kublar's suite. The door was already open, but he still knocked.

"Good morning."

Dr. Kublar answered him from somewhere. "Come in Edward and help yourself to breakfast. I'll be with you presently."

Eddie went into the main room where he'd been previously. He found Mu pouring a cup of coffee at a serving stand. He handed it over and gestured to the dining room through the open doors.

Eddie went into the dining room that was lit with candles and laid out elegantly with a setting at the ends of a long teak table. His name was on a place card at the one end. He took his seat. Mu was at his side placing a plate full of poached eggs, crisp bacon, potatoes, and a separate fruit compote in front of him. Under a newly arrived silver covered dish Eddie found French toast powdered with sugar. Mu added a tall glass of pulpy orange juice.

Eddie all of a sudden was famished. Ten minutes later he pushed the plates away, stuffed. Mu poured more coffee.

Dr. Kublar entered the room wearing an emerald green cloak; the gold threading glittered in the candlelight. He said good morning, took his seat at the other end of the table. Mu served him tea and a small, dark biscuit. Dr. Kublar put on tiny dark glasses. He ate the biscuit in two bites, but chewed extensively. Finally he touched his lips delicately with a napkin, sipped his tea noisily. His inscrutable smile seemed to contain all the mysteries of the Orient.

"Have you found employment yet, Edward?"

"No, sir. I'm not sure what to do. I could do phone soliciting again, I suppose. If you're worried about the rent—"

"I am not worried in the least, Edward, but I have a job offer, if you're interested. It is a little unusual. The pay is good and it involves travel."

"Really? Where to, and doing what?"

"To Honolulu, to meet with an associate of mine and deliver a package to him. Oh, nothing contraband, but highly valuable. An ancient Tablet that he will translate for me. You would stay a week, enjoy yourself, and then bring the Tablet and the translation back. Your work would be done in two brief meetings. Everything would be paid for. You would receive 2,000 dollars besides."

"Wow, how could I say no to that? When do I leave?"

"Today."

3

The hours rushed by and back from shopping Eddie packed: bathing trunks, suntan lotion, three short sleeve shirts, a backup pair of sunglasses. Eddie checked on his money stash. He had money in his wallet, a wad in his right pocket, and some large bills in an inner jacket pocket. He had rolled a few joints, and added them to some other items tied together: a razor, toothbrush, hairbrush, comb, and a shoehorn. He had a momentary feeling of panic imagining being arrested at the airport, but Mark had told him that he'd flown there and back a number of times holding with no problems, even carrying it on his person.

He was summoned to Dr. Kublar to pick up The Tablet which Eddie found was kept in a soft black leather case with a zipper. The Tablet itself was about the size of a shorthand notepad, grayish green, thin and surprising light. The weird script and symbols were so tiny he imagined a powerful magnifier would have to be used to decipher it.

"It can never be damaged," Dr. Kublar said with a satisfied air, as Eddie examined it. "And I hope Mr. Shoen is the man who can read it. He has been successful with other ancient tablets, however none like this."

Airborne once again Eddie looked down between cloud layers at the Pacific Ocean, ordered a gin tonic. The sharp rankness of captured cigarette smoke dominated the air in the cabin and stung his eyes; he flipped on the small overhead fan. He hand carried

Dr. Kublar's Tablet in a sealed manila envelope that sat in front of him in the webbed back seat holder along with airline safety instructions, the puke bag, and a magazine with a couple of pages torn out. Dr. Kublar had instructed him never to let the package out of his sight, so it would have to go with him to the bathroom as well. Immediately on arrival at the hotel he was to give it to a Mr. Shoen, who would show him a picture ID and say the code words: blue baby. Quite intriguing, Eddie thought, like the spy thriller he was reading. After a curious stringy, chicken dinner, and a few more pages of the novel he was reading, Eddie drifted off, the package securely behind him. He was awakened by the smiling, freckled stewardess making certain he was buckled up.

Outside on the tarmac the humid night air enveloped Eddie like a caress. He was thrilled to be here. He thought of his mother's Hawaiian obsession. Perhaps he was fulfilling it in some mythic family quest/journey way. He would surprise her with a postcard he thought, even though they were estranged. In the hotel lobby he and the others from the shuttle were greeted by a committee of good looking Hawaiian kids in short sleeve white polo shirts and khaki shorts. They welcomed the new arrivals, placed purple and white leis around each of their necks, and encouraged them to have some pineapple juice served in paper cups lined up on a table. They were around Eddie's age. One of the girls pouring the juice gave him the eye.

Mr. Shoen made himself known directly after Eddie checked in. In fact, he had followed him in, had watched his back, and everyone around him. He stopped Eddie at the elevator and introduced himself. Eddie said hello to a plump, bald Asian man maybe fifty in a seersucker suit with tiny eyes that were close together. He wore thick glasses, no tie, with a red carnation stuck in his lapel. They shook hands. Mr. Shoen showed him the proper ID, and repeated the code words. Eddie invited him up to his room. Once there Mr. Shoen looked concerned when Eddie emerged from the bathroom. There was a knock at the door: a bellhop with Eddie's luggage. Eddie tipped him and he left.

"But where is it?" Mr. Shoen gasped. "Not in your luggage I hope!"

Eddie took off his jacket, showed Mr. Shoen that he had it tucked under his belt pressed firm against his lower back. Mr. Shoen smiled took the package, and wrote down an "emergency number" on a blank card with an address, date, time to meet in one week to return the Tablet and deliver the translation. After Mr. Shoen left Eddie looked over the room. It was fairly posh. There was a complimentary bottle of wine, some flowers, a snack selection, and fruit on the table. His window looked out on an identical high-rise, hotel, and down many floors, a pool. The pool was surrounded by an area of foliage enhanced by pinpoint, luminous lighting. The water was mercurial in the night, and appeared to almost pulse. Eddie peeled off his clothes, stepped into the spacious, modern shower. The marble and clear glass contours of the bathroom deserved to be called a work of art, he thought. He luxuriated under the warm pounding water, and later, still feeling restless, went out for an evening stroll.

Eddie was pleased to be in Honolulu. He wandered through the International Marketplace along with other tourists and over to the nearby beach. He sat in the sand, thought about how he had come to be here, and then resumed his walk. He came across four curious boulders. On a plaque before them was some writing that claimed them to be "Wizard Rocks" and that they held magical healing properties. Four powerful, mysterious healers had visited pre-15th century, and before leaving had the people drag these boulders to the beach which they transferred "mana" to. Eddie put his hands on one, and let his mind drift. Just when he was about to let go a silky ghost voice spoke in his head encouraging him to continue...."Wait...Just, a little, longer..." So he did, and in increments he felt a pleasing tingle beginning in his fingers, then overtaking his hands, traveling up his arms, and becoming almost a massage. He could not let go. He was startled at first when it roamed over his chest, then he saw an explosion of stars in his head—he thought maybe it was an acid flashback. He had doubted the reality of such a phenomena, but was now reconsidering. He could still not release his hands, and the voice was cooing: "...Relax...please, Eddie...relax, there...there... Enjoy..." and soon his whole body felt blissful...he was transforming into something like a god. He was awestruck, rushing with pleasure, a kaleidoscope of colors and patterns exploding behind his eyelids and then, it all stopped.

He was back to normal except for a slight motion sickness that passed when he released and raised his hands.

Something however was different, and of that Eddie was sure. What, he didn't know. He put his hands back on the stones, and as he suspected, nothing happened. He walked on, stunned at what had occurred. He felt an overall boost in energy, and aliveness. Everything seemed exaggerated. After walking along the empty stretch of beach, still in a kind of trance he came across a tiki hut bar set off by itself with slightly swaying palm trees on either side. A fearsome black tiki head stood above the entrance. On either side of a beaded curtain entrance were two others. A few lit torches led the way while others were stuck willy nilly in the sand surrounding the place. It drew him in like a dream.

Inside, Eddie thought it looked like the set for all the tropical, exotic adventure stories he'd ever read and loved as a boy, or the set for a teenage surfer movie. Bamboo was everywhere, with more tiki heads, more torches, thatch roofs over the bar and some booths in the back. The barkeep was a monkey faced character wearing a little black cap tilted to one side and a wide red and white striped jersey. He was polishing a glass. He nodded at Eddie and asked him what his pleasure was. Eddie ordered a beer. He didn't really want one, but he felt he had to order something, since he wanted to sit a while. Some strange notion told him that this bartender or this place had something to tell him or show him.

"Did ya just arrive?"

"I did," Eddie said, "My first time here. It's a wonderful place."

"There's a dark side to these sunny isles though, ya'know," the bartender said leaning in, and speaking low, although there was no one else around that Eddie could see. But then he heard coughing coming from one of the hidden booths.

"Well, sure. There's a dark side to everything isn't there?"

"Depends on your definition, why not tell me yours?"

"Why not tell me yours since you brought it up?"

"Fair enough." The bartender laughed, showed a wicked smile. "Or I could show'ya."

What a character Eddie was thinking. Why had he been drawn into this place? How could he be shown?

"How can you show me?" Eddie asked, trying the beer.

"Take a look outta that window over there." He gestured across the room. Eddie went over to the portal window with his beer. He peered out and seconds later jumped back. "What the fuck!" He had spilled some beer. He stood there looking at the bartender with his beer sloshing, his jaw hanging. Eddie had seen a creature looking back at him that at once registered to be something not of this world. Regaining his senses he looked again: nothing; prank? Too elaborate. He set down his beer, went outside, looked around, but the creature was gone. However a weird smell lingered for a moment, a smell that he had no reference for. The creature had been hairless, with deep, heavily shadowed black eyes that had a gold electric light dead center. Those eyes had sent a shiver through him. The skin was bluish white, with ridges on the forehead, a missing nose. It's fantastic mouth reminded him of Aztec priest skulls he'd seen pictures of, but this mouth was fluid, alive, and a black viper's tongue had shot out, retracted. He hadn't seen the rest of the body, but the expression had been so startling he doubted his sanity.

Eddie felt as though he was one of the last surviving persons on some lost and deranged planet. He stood there on the beach in the crazy moonlight. The sea stretched out like some Lovecraftian entity of its own and seemed to call to him, to draw him into its arms, into its waves and waters that lulled, and crashed. The moon and stars seemed to beam a kind of energy into him. He was re-experincing the feeling from the Wizard Stones while whirls of colors unfurled around him. He fell to his knees in the sand. A kind of fit came over him. He rolled to his side, his body convulsing, shivering. Moments later he sat up, recovered. Monkeys appeared from somewhere leaping all around chattering, showing their teeth. The monkey faced bartender was there too, grinning. Eddie got to his feet, a whirl of sea wind blew the barkeep and his monkeys away. More hallucinations?

Still awestruck he reluctantly decided to go back into the bar, but it was no longer there. Not there at all, just sand and one bedraggled palm tree. Surely some kind of acid flashback he thought, because what else could it be? He turned and made his way back down the beach toward the hotels, yet as he walked he could see no signs of life, no buildings, nothing. He stopped. The voice in his head spoke again instructing him to close his eyes. He did and heard a roaring sound approaching. The voice commanded him to keep his eyes shut. The roaring came closer, became louder, louder, then he felt a fierce wind that he had to steady himself not to be moved by. It passed, the voice said: now, and he opened his eyes to again see the hotels, lights, some people on the beach, traffic passing by. Eddie turned around, looked to where the tiki bar had been, but it was still only empty beach.

The bar in the hotel lobby was empty, yet open. Eddie ordered a gin tonic, a double, took it over to a booth against a wall. Half way through the drink he was calming down, yet still trying to understand what had happened. Was he having some kind of psychotic breakdown? Brain tumor? It started with the Wizard Stones, or did it start with meeting Dr. Kublar? And what of Mr. Shoen and the Tablet? Had he been drugged? How had he ended up in the curious state and situation? What in the world was happening to him?

Eddie felt as though he'd wandered into a fantastic tale of fiction, or some mind bending spiritual derangement episode. Should he see a doctor? Best wait and see. He felt okay now finishing the drink. Eddie noticed that someone was standing over him: the cute girl, the pourer of the pineapple juice. She was with a friend equally as pretty. Eddie stood, said hi and asked if they would care to join him. The friend looked at her wristwatch, said that she had to go back to work. The girl who remained, who was named Soma already had a glass of wine in her hand, and soon had a hand on Eddie's arm. They relaxed and were soon telling each other a bit about themselves.

After another drink they ended up in Eddie's room. Soma turned out to be a handful, and performed a vampy strip tease. Eddie marveled over her smooth, brown skin. He submerged himself in her caresses and hot kisses. Afterward they lay together. She looked into his eyes, asked: "We're best friends now?" Eddie said yeah, asked if she would like to get high. He filled the oversized bathtub with bubble bath. They slid in, smoked a joint, sipped mineral water, a while later they were back in bed.

The following day Soma had a list of things Eddie should see and do while he was here. First they went first to the Waikiki Aquarium. In wonderment Eddie studied the varied marine life of the South Pacific. He was dazzled, and the joint of Soma's Maui Wowie they'd smoked on the way enhanced it threefold. They grabbed a snack, and next were off to Hanauma Bay where they snorkeled among the multicolored reef fish. They were searching for the state fish: the humuhumunakunukuapuaa. Soma tugged at his arm. He turned and saw two of them: snubby nosed, bright little buggers. Soma wanted to go to the Dole Plantation, the word's largest maze, but Eddie was thinking about a rest, and getting back in the sack with her. But when he said he was a little bushed she only laughed, and told him that now was the time to push himself. Eddie knew the wisdom of that, having practiced that outlook himself, and so his whole demeanor, and his whole energy level transformed. Soma was pleased, but had changed her mind, and now wanted to visit the Manoa Falls. "We'll dream under the canopy of a tropical forest. Would you like that?"

At days end they arrived back at the hotel, and as they passed through the lobby Soma asked Eddie if he would like to hike Diamond Head, and also see the Botanical Gardens tomorrow, and— Eddie cut her off whispering in her ear as they approached the elevator: "I want to explore Somaland." She laughed, squeezed his hand as they entered the elevator. When they turned around Eddie saw Mr. Shoen walking by just as the door closed. In the room he called the front desk to see if he had any messages. He didn't. He told Soma about his job here, that he was awaiting the translation of an ancient Tablet. Soma said the man he spotted was probably at the hotel for some other reason, especially since it had only been a day. That made sense. Eddie was pleased that things were making sense again. He still thought about his wild experiences, and wondered if it could happen again, but he kept that to himself.

When evening came Soma transformed herself into a goddess. She wore a silvery, short dress that plunged in the back. Her face was so artfully made up it made him think she must be a reincarnated queen. They walked to a hall a few blocks away, and had dinner followed by a spectacular Polynesian show. The week flew by with Soma as his guide, driver, lover and companion, but the day she did not show up was the same day he was to meet Mr. Shoen. He decided to give him a call. Shoen sounded surprised, then indignant, and said that of course he had finished the translation. Eddie explained that his flight out was for the following morning, and that he was just a little nervous. He invited him to dinner at the hotel. Mr. Shoen could not make it, nor did he want Eddie to come to him. He wanted to meet at the original arranged meeting place, at the agreed on time, by the Wizard Stones.

That gave Eddie pause and when he asked why there, or why not somewhere else, Mr. Shoen said he was in a hurry and hung up. Eddie called Soma and found that her number had been disconnected with no forwarding number. Eddie looked out the window across to an identical building. The small balconies gave the whole structure the presence of a giant hive. He had been in the mood to get high, but now he wasn't. Instead he was on edge. He spent the rest of the day by the pool, hoping Soma would show up. She didn't. He finished off the Trevanian novel, spent some time swimming, sun bathing, hanging out at the swim-up bar sipping juice, and talking with a fit older woman, who was a travel writer. As the day neared end he finally had a gin Martini, which he drank quickly. He decided to try the hotel's restaurant for dinner. He kept thinking of his rendezvous with Mr. Shoen, how strange it was, and Soma's disappearance, her disconnected number. He decided to call Mr. Shoen again, to try one last time to entice him into dinner or at least a drink, but when he had the call put through, he found Mr. Shoen's number had been disconnected as well.

4

Right before sunset Eddie arrived at the beach in a troubled state that he tried to talk himself out of, telling himself that he was only getting carried away, having read so many novels of fantasy, espionage, the supernatural, and that Mr. Shoen would have a perfectly reasonable explanation for the disconnected phone. He looked at the card Mr. Shoen had given him. He arrived at the correct address at the agreed upon time. He looked at The Wizard Stones but he didn't approach them. A couple of Japanese girls were taking photographs of each other posing by them. Eddie had picked up a pack of cigarettes earlier since he found smoking helpful in difficult circumstances. He hadn't had much of an appetite, and a bit of a headache from the sun and over thinking the situation. The cigarette wasn't helping. After only a couple of drags of a second one he gave the pack to a beach bum who was trying to sell him some sloppy watercolors in bamboo frames. There was one Eddie sort of liked of a tiki head. A few minutes later he thought he should have bought it, since the price had been so low and the artist so friendly. He looked down the street, but the beach bum was long gone. The sunset was already looking to be spectacular with wide swirls of orange and a background of a trailing luminous yellow in a royal blue of sky that was gradually turning darker, but he wasn't enjoying it much. Instead he was anticipating the arrival of Mr. Shoen.

Fifteen minutes passed, then twenty, a half hour. Eddie was

checking the passersby carefully. He leaned against a wall, wished he had kept the cigarettes. A bad feeling grew worse by the minute. Long before an hour was up he knew Mr. Shoen wasn't coming, but still he found a spot to sit to wait some more, although he knew it was futile. After another twenty minutes, feeling miserable he started to walk away—then he saw him! Not Mr. Shoen, but Mark, his ex-partner in crime in Berkeley. Mark was crossing the street. He looked different: he had a serious tan, was wearing a snappy tea colored straw brim hat, and a rumpled, beige, lightweight suit. Following his intuition Eddie decided to follow him rather than make himself known. He followed him down a number of back streets. At the end a long alley Eddie watched him look around before ducking into a back entrance of a warehouse. Eddie waited a bit, found the door unlocked and went in too.

He heard voices, held back a moment, and then proceeded down a semi-dark hallway. At the end some light was falling across the hallway from a back office. The voices were louder, but echoing so he couldn't really understand the conversation. He could make out snippets, some words, something about "a buyer" something about "a backup". A deeper voice said: "The Goddamn thieving Japs!" "Beat 'em at their own game," a female voice added, and Eddie recognized something especially familiar about that voice. It sounded like Soma. He had to get a look. He crept closer, and when he could see into the deep room converted into office spaces he was shocked. Mark sat on a wooden chair the opposite way with his hat tilted back. Mr. Shoen sat at a desk, and Soma sat on top of another desk with her shapely legs crossed in front of her. Eddie ducked back, wondering just what the hell was going on.

He listened some more but couldn't decipher much. They were arguing, but keeping their voices low most of the time. Eddie found a good spot behind some boxes to hide. They came out a little later, went down the hallway and out. Eddie made his way to the office door, but found it locked. He crept back to the street entrance, and looked out a side window. It was clear, they were gone. He found a board, went back to the office and slammed it through the glass. He cleared away the jagged parts, stuck his arm in, opened the door. They had left one dim light on, and there was some light coming from a street lamp. Eddie was going on instinct, knowing that there were too many coincidences. He was in a panic at losing the Tablet, but now he felt he might be able to get it back. The desk Shoen had been sitting at was an old gray metal number. All its drawers were locked. He was stumped on what to do next when his inner antenna directed him to a nearby bookshelf. There three, gray tiki heads sat looking ominous in the near dark. Behind the middle one he found a set of keys. Back at the desk he began to go through the drawers. He didn't find anything of interest except a .38 revolver that he decided to leave alone. His instinct urged him to look closer at the deepest drawer: a drawer similar to one where he and Mark had made their score. Still nothing of interest, then he felt about at the top. Something was taped there. He pulled it down and couldn't believe his eyes: Dr. Kublar's Tablet.

 Eddie left quickly, walking fast, his heart pumping. He heard his name, turned to see Mark running toward him from the end of the alley. Eddie flagged a cab before he could get to him. In something of a panic he checked out of his hotel, went out a back entrance, took a bus downtown where he checked into another hotel, a shabby one. The desk clerk was a fat Islander wearing a T-shirt featuring the famous surfer, and beach boy Duke Kahanamoku. He looked to be in a foul mood, the clerk, not Duke. He mopped some sweat off his forehead with a handkerchief. He threw down a clipboard holding a registration form for Eddie to fill out. He lit a cigarette, breathing heavily, and looking at Eddie without expression. His new room was barren, windowless, and beat. It looked like a set for a tawdry scene of some sort. He didn't unpack. Instead he sat on the wobbly chair and waited. Sounds of rough sex leaked through the thin wall, and tried to ignore the sharp, harsh smell that seemed to permeate the room. He thought about changing rooms, but decided against it. Instead he went out for some air, the Tablet pressing against his back. He decided to call Dr. Kublar. After a couple of rings, Mu picked up.

"Mu, it's Eddie in Honolulu. Is the doctor there? It's important."

"Yes, Mr. Eddie. I get."

Eddie waited impatiently. Finally Mu was back. "He sleep, coming now..."

"Yes, Edward, what is it? No problem I hope."

Eddie rushed through what had transpired in bits and spurts, Dr. Kublar stopping him at times to elaborate, clarify, finally said: "Edward I believe you've been sent to me. My advice is to stay in your new room for the most part, and be careful getting your flight out. I'll contact someone there to make sure you're not molested. And Mu will meet you here when you arrive."

The following morning Eddie splurged on a cab to the airport. He was cautious about who might be watching him. He didn't see Mr. Shoen, Soma or Mark anywhere, so he checked in. How did Mark become involved in this? Coincidence? Eddie bought a copy of The Honolulu Advertiser and hid behind it in a corner of the waiting area. As the time to board drew nearer the urge to urinate came over him since he'd had too much Kona coffee. He looked over the top of the newspaper. The coast looked clear.

The restroom was empty. As he was coming out of the stall Mark was standing there smiling like the devil wearing the same suit and hat and holding a wicked looking blade. "Give me the fucking Tablet now and I'll let you live, for old time's sake." Someone else was coming in. Mark shoved Eddie back into the stall, but then Mark was collapsing as a young Chinese man had shoved his way in. He had glossy slicked back hair, and wore a gray shark skin suit, and leather form fitting gloves. He held a syringe he'd stuck Mark with. The man pocketed Mark's weapon. "Help me Edward," he said and the two of them put Mark on the toilet seat then they left. "Mr. Rabbit," he said by way of introduction, and shook Eddie's hand. He slid on a pair of aviators. "You're flight is boarding. Go now. Best of luck and give my warmest regards to the doctor."

Eddie's heart was still thumping, his mind was still whirling as he watched the rapidly passing tarmac, felt the plane lifting off. Was his life to be one escape after another? The fantastic elements were blowing his mind. Would Mark have cut him, stabbed him? He believed he would have. And Soma, was she there only to keep an eye on him? Why? Mr. Shoen had the Tablet, but she had convinced him not to contact Mr. Shoen, or seek him out. And Mark? And the voice? And the alien at the Tiki Hut Bar. The whole thing was crazy, mind bending, freaky and far out. Eddie was glad to be on his way back to the mainland.

It was cool in San Francisco when his flight arrived. A few sunburned passengers were hugging themselves against the change in temperature, struggling with their awkward boxes of pineapples. Mu was waiting, wearing a dark winter coat, and a fedora that hid his pigtail. Snug in a specially devised seat and an extended pedal system, Mu drove them back to the city in the doctor's 1953 black Buick Special that smelled of new leather upholstery. For the most part they both remained silent. Eddie felt some sanity returning and had Mu stop at a supermarket to pick up some provisions.

Mu stopped the old Buick at Dr. Kublar's building entrance. He had to park the car in a garage on Nob Hill. Eddie stepped out, grabbed his bag, and the groceries from the back seat. Inside was the familiar smell of incense that too he found reassuring. Tacked to his door was a small brown envelope and once inside Eddie opened it. Dr. Kublar wanted him immediately on arrival to come to his apartment with the Tablet. He headed upstairs. He was about to knock when he heard Mu running lightly up the steps. He arrived not the least out of breath, opened the door with a skeleton key. "Wait prease." Mu directed Eddie to a bench in the hallway. The floor as well as the walls were covered in a mixture of Persian, Turkish and Oriental rugs. Eddie heard voices. Mu was back in his regular attire directing Eddie to a room he'd never seen before.

Dr. Kublar was sitting up in an impressive four poster bed with a canopy that looked like a place one might smoke opium. Eddie handed the Tablet over. Dr. Kublar nodded at a chair for Eddie to take. The doctor removed it from its soft leather cover, rubbed his hands over it, murmuring something under his breath, and looking at it as one might look into a crystal ball. He held it to his chest, then he placed it on the other side of him.

"Welcome back Eddie. You did a marvelous job. It is a miracle it was not lost. You have intuitive powers, of that there is no doubt. You were sent to me, and of that I am sure."

Eddie was not sure what he meant but it sounded good. He had questions.

"Dr. Kublar you did warn me that the mission could be dangerous, but how is it that my old associate Mark Sullivan was part of it? And what happened exactly? I thought you trusted Mr. Shoen?"

"Money does strange things to people Edward. A certain Japanese mogul offered Shoen more than he could ever refuse, but then tried to cut it down. I would say a kind of destiny was in play regarding your old friend, or associate as you say. Tell me more."

Eddie stumbled a bit telling him how he and Mark had worked together, and saw a flicker in the doctor's eye. He switched topics to his experience with the wizard stones, the voice, the bar, and the creature he had witnessed. When he was finished Dr. Kublar clapped his hands twice to call Mu. Dr. Kublar spoke to him in Mandarin when he entered the room. Mu bowed slightly, departed silently.

"Edward, that is the voice of the guardian, your distant guardian. By becoming part of the Tablet's history, and with the correct intentions you have achieved first level entry and protection. Oh, it's not foolproof, but a powerful ally for you and your own personal path."

Eddie was trying to comprehend that; it did ring true with him somehow. He was thrilled that this new life he had walked into was an unfolding mystery. It was beginning to create a new kind of logic for him. Mu came back into the room with a tea tray, an ornate teapot, two matching cups, saucers. Next to the cups were small black balls that looked like tar. Eddie knew that it was opium.

"Let's celebrate the return of the Tablet, and this will give us long and sweet dreams, and keep the chill at bay."

They swallowed the opium, sipped tea, and continued to talk, although Dr. Kublar did most of the talking. Eddie became gradually hypnotized with his extravagant tales and lazy style. Mu, sat in a corner of the room on a cushion writing in a notebook. When the opium came on Eddie felt a warmness spread throughout his body, his heart beating with waves of slow pleasure, and well being. He began to lose track of Dr. Kublar's narrative: something about riding elephants in a lost jungle, coming across an enchanted forgotten village populated by a blind albino race who'd developed wing like appendages under their arms. Eddie steadied himself and listened to Dr. Kublar's voice, ancient and wise.

"I met with the leader who claimed to be two hundred years old. He taught me many things. He and his people could fly but not very high and only for short distances. They had developed bat like echolocation expertise over time as well."

Eddie began to nod off again, Dr. Kublar's words became the

background sound like a slow moving river. Eddie saw himself floating on a black lacquered barge down that drowsy river....
   a pleasant hum of motor propelled the craft at a crawl...a pale gigantic moon...twinkling of stars hanging over head...the planets whirling slowly from time to time...then Mu was shaking his arm, his cat smile: "Timey for sleep Mr. Edward. Timey for dream." Edward looked over to Dr. Kublar—he had rolled over on his side, was snoring lightly. As Eddie lay down on his own bed he continued his journey down the river that had shifted to morning's golden light...the water so clear it looked false—changed by the rising sun...the dappled frond's shadows, an Impressionist painting coming to life...a frog...green glass becoming water...reflecting enormous lilies...floating by these enchanted grottos...passing by in a boyhood pleasure dream....

5

The next day Eddie was still a bit dopey. He pushed himself to get into the shower, then languished under the pounding hot water until he felt fine. He made coffee with Mark's old percolator, toasted some sourdough bread, flipped a couple of eggs, and poured a glass of orange juice. Outside his window the pagoda roof appeared somber in the gray dawn. He relived the whole crazy week in his mind. He was beginning to feel his feet back on ground. Opium was a magical drug he decided, but, he also knew of its dangers: abuse led to addiction. Dr. Kublar explained that a specific amount of time must be allotted each time a person indulges. He said: "This can be done with a person who is in control of their habits and routines, or one who has learned by bitter experience. For each it's different, but a good rule is to never partake more than twice per month. And, if you are injured, or ill and need pain medication take the opiod that is prescribed. Never use the O, since it is sacred. Always note in your calendar the date you took it." Eddie thought about all that while eating his breakfast, and gazing at the pagoda.

Eddie looked in his closet wondering what to wear. He had dressed down for Hawaii in a casual cotton sports coat, lightweight slacks, and Converse low-cuts. He had picked up a few tapered white, short sleeve shirts, some T-shirts, and a thin gray and white striped cardigan for a switch in the evenings. He had ended up wearing a pair of army style khaki shorts, T-shirts, canvas hat, and flip flops most of the time though. Now with pleasure he put on the trousers of an exquisitely tailored dark blue and purple striped velvet suit with large silver buttons. He slipped on his highly polished Beatle boots, a black mock turtle neck completed the ensemble. He put the jacket on, looked at himself in the mirror. The island tan with the Mod clothes was strange at first, but then he warmed up to it, and added some blue eye shadow. "blue baby" he said out loud.

Outside Eddie felt fresh, and invigorated. He took some deep breaths, and took in his surroundings. He contemplated a story he might write: A Mod in Chinatown. He was to visit Richmond in the Haight today. Overhead a red banner covered in Chinese lettering hung across the alleyway announcing something or another. It was connected to the herb shop across the way. Eddie went over to the shop, always delighted with olfactory pleasures, the haunted, medicinal smells of these curious shops. The owner, wearing a skull cap, a fuzzy wool jacket, and an apron, was sweeping up. Eddie stood in the doorway, and asked what the banner said. The shopkeeper came over in small, mincing steps. He looked at the banner as if seeing it for the first time himself. "New ginseng. Best ginseng. Only Kim Kim has." He pointed to two barrels full, and above them over the counter was a young Chinese face that Eddie hadn't seen amongst the stacked boxes and jars that crowded the countertop. Eddie winked at the youth. The boy's expression remained unchanged. Little bugger Eddie thought. Eddie noticed a curious stone head among great piles of Chinese newspapers and string tied brown packages at the far end of the counter, all looking forgotten and from another era entirely. The head was ancient, mysterious, and foreboding. It seemed to speak to Eddie. He asked the shopkeeper if it was for sale. Kim Kim looked at it, then back at Eddie with a quizzical expression. "Not real. Fake. Only ten dollah." Eddie took out his wallet, and paid him. Kim Kim dusted, and then wrapped the head even though Eddie asked him not to. He bought some of the ginseng too. Kim Kim snickered, made a fucking motion. He wrapped the ginseng too. He motioned with his arm as a huge penis and laughed. He showed Eddie a statue of a large wooden penis behind a curtain.

After taking the heavy head back to his apartment Eddie was off to the Haight. He flagged a cab on California Street that swerved in traffic to get to him. A cable car operator yelled at him, calling him a moron. The cabbie, a old tough as nails character swore back at the operator, and flipped him the bird. Eddie laughed. The driver looked at him in the rear view mirror. "Those assholes think they rule the thoroughfares. They don't, those goddamn pricks!"

Arriving a little early at Haight and Asbury Eddie decided to look around. Each time he visited though he found the place a little seedier. He noticed more closed up shops, the smell of piss, and riff raff moving in. A fantastic jewelry shop he planned to visit was not only closed up, there was a pile of black shit, half smeared in the entranceway. He'd nearly stepped in it, but was saved at the last minute. He peered back into the entranceway and said fuck. A tough looking lady, maybe an aging biker chick, was standing nearby waiting for the bus. She laughed at Eddie's reaction. "They're worse than pigs huh?" Eddie said yeah, and continued onward to Richmond's place. He still had a little time to kill, and bought some paraphernalia at a head shop.

Richmond welcomed Eddie into the old Victorian. Eddie looked into the room where he had tripped on his last visit. The lighting was still dim. There were a few people kicking back listening to The Seeds, a group Eddie liked as well. He followed Richmond into the kitchen in the rear of the house. On the kitchen table a variety of drugs were laid out on the clean white surface. An attractive girl sat at one end rolling a spliff from a tray shaped like a fig leaf. She winked at Eddie. Richmond introduced them.

Her name was Alice and Eddie felt a spark right off. He hoped she wasn't Richmond's girlfriend. Richmond said:

"Eddie my man have you ever seen such a fine presentation? Here we have the buds of primo Panama Red, weed you will fall in love with, and cry when it is gone. Next is Lebanese hash that will blow your socks off." Alice grinned, and fired up the spliff she'd expertly rolled.

"These are magic mushrooms from Oaxaca, and here, Orange Sunshine from the Brotherhood of Eternal Love man, here some fine Peruvian flake, and this my friend is a special treat that is rarely found anymore: Chinese opium. Are you impressed?"

"I am awed," Eddie said taking the spliff that Alice handed him and a seat at Richmond's invitation. Richmond sat as well, and looked over his goods as Henry VIII might've gloated over an extravagant feast.

"Now Eddie which would you like to sample, and/or purchase?"

Eddie still had some pot, but thought he could buy some more. The ball of black opium was like a magnet to him. Richmond eye's seemed to glint for a second. He shared a quick look with Alice who was cleaning off a round mirror. They watched her sprinkle a good portion of coke from a bindle, make six lines with a razor blade, and snort one in each nostril with a plastic straw. She passed it to Eddie who was not really fond of the drug. Nevertheless to not appear dull snorted his two, and passed it to Richmond who to Eddie's surprise passed. He said that it interfered with his pot high. Alice laughed. Eddie wished he had passed too, but, on the other hand Alice was smiling at him in a most encouraging way and offering one of Richmond's lines.

"Eddie, my band is debuting tonight, can you come?'

"Sure. I'd love to," Eddie said, and reluctantly snorted the extra line. "What's the name?"

"Wolf Snake."

"Nice."

"This house is your house, you're welcome to spend the day and enjoy yourself. Maybe you can help with loading some of the equipment tonight?"

"My casa your casa amigo," Alice said with a chuckle.

"Thanks." Eddie felt his heart beat accelerate from the coke, his mouth going dry. He looked at Alice, she seemed cool as a kitten, and was rolling up small balls of opium she'd come up with from somewhere. She asked Richmond if he had smoked any. He said that he'd cooked some at the stove on a hot knife. He had sucked up the smoke, but felt that unless you had the proper pipe, eating it was better. Eddie agreed, said that a hot cup of tea is best to get it activated, and an even preferred way of taking it by many. They both looked at him a little surprised.

"So you've tried it before?" Richmond asked.

"Yes, and I found it most pleasurable." He went on to echo the the danger of over indulgence while thinking to himself that he ought to follow his own advice, since a little later he found himself swallowing a ball along with them, and having some English tea. Richmond decided he wanted to take a drive around the city to burn off some steam. He offered to play the role of chauffeur for Eddie and Alice. Alice loved the idea and squealed with pleasure.

"I'll bring this along," she said picking up the spliff that was only half smoked. Eddie and Alice met Richmond out front. Richmond pulled up in a 1967 emerald green/black top Cadillac Sedan DeVille right out of Matt Helm.

"Isn't he too much," Alice said and to Eddie's delight she had taken his arm.

"So you and Richmond aren't a couple?"

"A couple? What an old fashioned idea. Let's trip tonight eh Eddie?"

"Sure, sure," he said, watching her jump ahead of him, open

the back door for him and bow.

"In, in sir," she laughed.

Richmond proceeded to race around the city. They visited Golden Gate Park, and foggy Ocean Beach where they finished off the spliff. They became tangled in traffic both downtown and at Fisherman's Wharf. Finally Richmond said he'd had enough and needed to get ready for the show. Alice had crashed and was snoozing on Eddie's arm. Back at the house Alice went off somewhere. Eddie followed Richmond downstairs to a pre-show rehearsal. The room had cardboard egg cartons on the walls and ceiling. The drums were set up and the other members whom Eddie hadn't met were sitting on high stools tuning up in front of their amplifiers. Pitts, who looked something like Graham Parsons was playing bass. Diamond Jack, the guitarist greatly resembled Keith Richards. Jack was from Liverpool and spoke with such a thick accent it was hard to understand him. Eddie was told that there was a second guitarist who was still at his straight job. Matt, the singer whom he'd met, was walking back and forth smoking a cigarette.

Richmond came barreling down the steps saying, "Let's go mates! Work out the kinks! He sat behind his kit, twirled his sticks Keith Moon style, started a kind of tribal beat. Pitts coaxed out a bass line that before long turned rumbling. Diamond Jack opened up with a squall of biting licks before settling into a rhythm that reminded Eddie of a Sonics number: The Witch. Matt grabbed his mike. He looked serious and wild. He began and his soulful, slightly ragged voice howled with emotion and filled the room. The tune: I Live on High Street would become one of Eddie's favorites from their set.

After a bite to eat, conversation, smoking some hash with Matt, Diamond Jack and Alice (who was now wearing a motorcycle jacket) they gathered out front and loaded up Pitts's VW van. The other guitarist had joined them: Cooper, who looked clean cut, could've been a Beach Boy, turned out to be a cheerful guy who took no drugs, but was quite a drinker. Before the night was out he and Diamond Jack would drink themselves into a stupor.

The gig was at The Palms, an all around hangout for hipsters at night, a coffee shop by day. After the equipment was set up Alice asked Eddie to join her back in the van for a hit of C. He thanked her, but passed, admitted that he wasn't crazy about coke—a blast once in a blue moon was about all he was up for. She didn't look disappointed but asked: "How about the O? You like that though huh?" Eddie liked her, but considering Richmond's assessment of her as "too wild" he was having second thoughts about trying to get to know her. Although she professed to being against monogamous relationships he didn't quite believe her. He said : "Yeah, I must be careful with that drug. Best to stick to ganja mostly."

"But it's boring to be careful."

"That's your view, not mine. Call me crazy, but when I cross the street I look both ways. "

He took his wallet out, and extracted two tabs of Orange Sunshine. Alice smiled and they both dropped. She leaned up and kissed him on the cheek. There were only a handful of others in the club. The music played over the sound system was familiar to Eddie as the Beau Brummells. Alice said:

"Hey, let's get out of here. It's dreary at this hour. Next they'll be doing a sound check which is boring as fuck. My friend Maggie doesn't live far from here, and if she's not at home I have a key."

Alice had stepped into the light, already looking seriously stoned to Eddie. He wondered if the acid had been such a great idea. He decided to keep an eye on her best he could until they peaked and leveled off.

"Sounds groovy...but should we tell Richmond?"

"No, no, he's busy. We'll come back for the show. We um have hours baby."

They walked hand in hand down a Polk Street that to Eddie started to take on the aura of an enormous aquarium. People looked to be swimming or sailing rather than walking. A black man with his mouth wide open, but making no sound, arms to his side, looked like a slow moving torpedo. Eddie stopped to get a grip. Alice laughed, rested an arm on his shoulder. On Sutter Street at a weathered apartment building they climbed three floors, falling into each other a couple of times, laughing, and finally making it to the door. There was no answer to their knocks. In they went to find a stylish, comfy pad. Alice threw open the curtains, and it was as through a burst of stars appeared, turned to tiny fragments and fell in slow motion. Eddie was peaking. Alice was a sorceress, a witch he decided and he wanted to make love to her, but, he couldn't feel his body. He was sprawled out on the floor on a lush Persian carpet, his head resting against the couch. Everything was melting.

Alice found the stereo, placed an album on the turntable and sang something to herself. Eddie listened to an echo, to a sustained distortion. His eyes were closed. He was watching a squadron of what looked like electronic humming birds maneuvering in a alien landscape of clear pink rocks that began growing until they obliterated everything in their path. Eddie forced his eyes open to a near naked Alice well into something like the dance of the seven veils. Eddie couldn't identify the music, but it invoked a mysterious, Middle Eastern mood with a steady hypnotic drumming, maybe an oud or a sitar—he couldn't tell everything was so out of whack. Alice was dancing like one possessed, lost in delirium. Eddie loved it. When they did finally make love it was like they'd been doing it for a long time, and knew each other well.

Alice rolled over onto on her stomach, her bare legs in the air, watching the TV without sound: James Cagney was roughing up some hood. It seemed to Eddie that many, many hours had passed. He regretted missing the band, but Alice who carried a gold pocket watch like the rabbit in Wonderland declared that Wolf Snake should be taking the stage soon, and that they should get dressed. Eddie was stunned at the time distortion. He started to think about time travel, and his experience in Honolulu again as he took a long mystical piss. Alice attended to her face in the mirror but so briefly that it would put many attractive girls to shame.

When they entered the club they found it packed. Wolf Snake was taking the stage for an healthy, enthusiastic crowd. Alice plowed through the people dragging Eddie along. She received no resistance, the crowd parted as though it was part of some previously arranged maneuver. To the side of the stage and by a huge speaker they stood. Eddie soon felt consumed, lifted, and baptized in sound. Alice was dancing wildly, a rock 'n roll sprite from some parallel universe where creatures had boundless energy and glee, or so Eddie thought. He made his way closer to the wall, and found a spot to lean, where he could still see the stage. Wolf Snake was a powerful group Eddie decided. They put on as good a show as Iggy and The Stooges.

6

A few days later Eddie gave Richmond a call, thanked him for the great night, and complemented him on the band's performance. Richmond said Wolf Snake was off to tour the Pacific Northwest and asked if Eddie would like to join them. He would have to pay his own way but, Richmond added:

"You'll stay high the whole time, get free admission and all the pussy you can handle. You could help out a little. Roadies usually do better than the band members. Lemme know by tonight so I can save you a ride. We have two cars and a van. You could ride with me."

Eddie thought for only seconds and said: "Yeah, count me in. Can you pick me up?" Richmond said they could and arrangements were made to meet at the Powell Street rear entrance of the Fairmont Hotel by the pharmacy. For some reason Eddie didn't want anyone to know exactly where he lived. It was like a private world to him.

"Oh, and Eddie, Alice wanted me to give you her number. You want it now or later?"

"Later." Eddie hung up and walked back through Chinatown, excited to be on the road again. He told Mu to inform Dr. Kublar he would be gone a few days. He began to pack a bag, but this time different gear: flash threads for the shows, and the parties afterward. As he was counting out some money there was a light tap on his door, a tap he had come to know: Mu.

Mu stood in the doorway, head slightly bowed, coughed to the side.

"Mr. Edward, the doctor would verly much like to have audience with you before your departure. Would you prease join himself for early dinner at 5 PM?"

"I'd be delighted," Eddie said and returned to packing. Eddie had been having dreams that he wanted to ask the doctor about since he'd studied dreamwork in Nepal with a master for a number of years. Eddie kept dreaming of the Tablet turning into a flickering screen of symbols, strange text whirling by endlessly, and different languages speaking in his head as though competing for his attention. Other dreams were the opposite. He was lying by an idyllic stream on a bank of soft grass. The voice was speaking to him in a soft tone that he believed, a voice that imbued great wisdom, and gave him specific instructions on how to move toward transformation. Yet, when he awoke, he couldn't remember the content.

Eddie sat back on his bed, closed his eyes, and watched the images and events swim back forth and throughout his mind. The one that finally surfaced was the recent time with Alice. He kept seeing that devilish, pixie smile of hers, remembering her soft skin, and touch, and the taste of her. He was getting an erection. Time for a wank.

He had begun reading one of the Castenada books that Mark, that bastard, had left behind. Eddie wondered if Mark had even read them or just had them because he thought they'd make him look hip. The books' way of thinking and views were completely different than anything he'd ever heard from Mark.

Again Eddie was led into Dr. Kublar's dining room. It was lit with candles that gave it the feeling of a seance, ritual or a secret meeting. Again he was served alone by Mu, who poured a glass of red wine. Mu lifted the silver lid cover of the meal. Eddie found many inviting items: sweet potatoes and apricots lightly sprinkled with bits of herb, green beans, with what he would learn later were thin strips of soy chicken in a black bean sauce, breakfast potatoes with tomato, mushroom, basil, the heads of baby bok choy in soy sauce, and brown rice sprinkled with roasted sunflower seeds. There was a basket of Moroccan crusty bread, still warm, and a small dish of black olives in oil. Eddie began enjoying the feast and didn't protest a lighter second helping. Finally Dr. Kublar entered the room dressed in a black cloak trimmed in silver around the collar, down the middle and on the cuffs. It made him appear a member of some ancient royalty. Mu served Eddie a small cup of black soup that he would learn was a Chinese dessert: sweet black sesame soup.

Dr. Kublar had the same thing he'd had on their last meeting: one biscuit and one cup of tea. Eddie imagined him gorging late at night in that opulent bed on something salty, or sugary until he felt sick. Then again, maybe not. Dr. Kublar was an enigma to Eddie. Instinctively he knew he was not his master, since Eddie didn't subscribe to that concept, but rather a teacher. Eddie had learned from others too: friends, artists, and creative thinkers, beginning with the wise old men of the pool hall. One particular hobo he'd spent talking with a few evenings before watching him hop a train out of Wormlysburg. And Eddie had learned much for himself, that is once he learned how to listen.

"Edward do you mind if we move into the study. I think it's the proper setting for our discussion this evening."

Dr. Kublar, in one fluid moment rose and glided over to Eddie. He offered his hand.

"Come my son."

The study was in a section of the flat that Eddie hadn't seen. He found it especially comfortable with velvet wing back chairs facing a low fire lightly crackling in a Edwardian fireplace. The walls were covered in black and white feather scroll wallpaper that brought Aubrey Beardsly to mind. There were three bookcases filled with hardbacks on every conceivable esoteric subject. Some of the tomes looked ancient, others of collected fables were gilt-edged. Eddie was thinking he would like to spend some afternoons in there browsing. He warmed his back standing by the fire. The chairs were moved closer to each other by Mu. Dr. Kublar sat and Mu extracted a footstool from underneath the chair that Dr. Kublar placed one tiny foot shod in a velvet slipper after the other on. Mu looked to Eddie, but he waved away the footstool offer. He sat and rubbed his hands together. Dr. Kublar spoke to Mu in Chinese who turned and left the room only to return a moment later with two brandies in snifters. Mu then returned to his seat across the room. Eddie sniffed the heady elixir, said cheers, prompting Dr. Kublar to say chin chin. They sipped the hundred year old brandy.

"Magnificent," said Eddie.

"So, Edward, come tell me of your new journey. Always exciting for me to hear since I mostly travel in my mind, or out of body."

"Out of body? Wow, could you tell me about that?"

"Edward you know all about it, come now. Didn't you want to really discuss dream work?"

Again Dr. Kublar had read Eddie's thoughts. He explained that telepathy was common place but mankind insisted on mystifying it. "Once one realizes that it exists, and is part of our makeup in the real world, then one begins to hone their skill in that area." Dr. Kublar talked more about dreams and how men of science scoffed at the idea that dreams meant anything at all. The doctor agreed that some of them are meaningless, but pointed out that most are forgotten too. "Now, the ones that are remembered, that continue to haunt, they should be examined closely. And persistent dream noting is a worthwhile practice for any artist. So, Edward let's hear the ones that concern you and I will give you my evaluation."

Eddie sniffed the brandy, took another sip, felt it move through him like a kind of time travel itself. "I've had reoccurring dreams of the Tablet, its flickering screen of symbols, and curious text that endlessly whirls through my mind. I hear different languages spoken from unseen entities. I feel they're speaking to me, but I can't understand them. Other times I dream of lying by an idyllic stream on a bank of soft grass. The voice begins speaking to me in a soft, encouraging tone. I believe the voice holds great wisdom, and it gives me specific instructions toward a transformation, or some psychological truth, psychic fulfillment, and yet when I awaken I can't remember them."

"You are now part of the family of the Tablet. You will continue with those dreams, as we all do. By the way I have found a new translator for the Tablet, located in Austin, Texas of all places. He will be here tomorrow night. When you return from your journey I hope to have something to share. The voice is your guardian, we call the distant guardian. The same voice you heard on the island. It is a voice coming from an underwater cave. If you note your dreams you will learn more, always. There is something stopping the guardian from completely allowing entrance. I sensed it when I first met you. Is there something troubling you? Something you feel you need to unburden yourself with?"

The meal and now the brandy had made Eddie very relaxed, yet he remained mostly alert from Dr. Kublar's formidable energy. It was as though there was an electric pulse coming from his mind and igniting Eddie's own, keeping him in the moment, and challenging him. Eddie threw caution to the wind and began:

"I was partner in a crime a while back and most strangely so, with Mark, the guy who led me to Mr. Shoen's warehouse. A very curious coincidence I thought. Together we robbed an upscale restaurant in the East Bay and took over twenty grand each. The job did not really qualify for my gentleman's crime criteria, but having lost my job, and feeling desperate to get above the scurrying for money crunch I went ahead with it."

Edward had been expecting a reprimand, disapproval but instead found the doctor laughing heartily.

"We will direct that criminal mindset of yours into a nobler pursuit, that is if you allow me to direct you. What if I told you that if you gave your portion back, your life would change for the better, and in ways you cannot imagine?"

"It's better to be broke and worrying about money, and taking dead end jobs to earn it?"

"You would not be broke, and money would be of little concern if you take the path I propose."

"I'm listening."

"Close your eyes."

Dr. Kublar took his hand. Eddie saw a wondrous sight: a bridge made of light under a rich blue sky, and to either side the tops of clouds. He walked on the bridge feeling blissful, feeling something beyond the highs he'd had on drugs or with sex, something beyond all of that: some magical region that was known yet unknown, and had always been waiting. He felt ecstasy rush through him, and found himself on the other side looking at the curious grottos that ran beside a great mountain. The air was crisp, his heartbeat was steady. He stepped down and into a pond, swimming as it spread out. He dove underwater, feeling vibrant. Eddie swam into the cave, and came up. He treaded water, steadily as he doggy paddled deeper into the cave, and saw a golden light. He swam with more purpose, and when he came into the light everything exploded into a prism of colors, sensations, fantastic, other worldly sounds, and he let go....

7

In the wee hours when Eddie woke up it was still dark. He felt transformed, ready for anything. He checked his preparations for his trip and wrote a note for Dr. Kublar:

"Dear Dr. Kublar, You are right. The voice is right. I will attend to it on my return. Thank you, Edward."

He felt an overall boost in his outlook, his morale, and his sense for adventure, as though a guidance system had been installed in his psyche that had been missing for far too long. His belief in the marvelous, chaos, the mysterious, as well as the rational now felt balanced. He went over the eight principles in his head: air, water, sun, nutrition, exercise, relaxation, moderation and spirituality. The last that could mean any vitally absorbing interest that uplifts one to another level of perception. Where had he learned this new philosophy? The voice thereof, via Dr. Kublar, the finest teacher he had ever encountered.

The black Sedan deVille glistened there under the street lamps, parked at the back entrance of the Fairmont Hotel. Eddie waved to Richmond and Diamond Jack, who were standing outside drinking coffee in Styrofoam cups, and smoking cigarettes. Eddie stowed his bag in the trunk, and climbed in the back to find Cooper sound asleep, drooling, leaning against a duffle bag. Before long they were on the highway, heading north, full of anticipation of new adventures. Cooper awoke, yawned, and wiped his face with his hand. Richmond turned to Diamond Jack, and said:

"So listen mate, that guitar bit you do on the break of Snatch?"

"Yea what ov it?"

"It's a little flowery isn't it? I remember you used to do a mean kinda Link Wray thing there."

"Er I thought the tune being about birds could ave a romantic like gitar bit more so?"

"Listen Jack, that rumble you do is best, it's what makes them crazy along with Mitch's voice. There will surely be a tune on the album that will require that kind of touch, but not "Snatch." Dig the lyrics: I gotta freaky momma. She's gotta do the rhumba. I'm a bone walkin' nodder, nodding to the Bast, lookin' at your snatch. Gotta gotta gotta get it... gonna gonna gonna lick it. Snaaaaaatch!

"Uh yeah mate, wat iz Bast?" queried Diamond Jack with a cockeyed look.

"Egyptian goddess of pleasure man," said Richmond.

"Personified by the cat, often portrayed as part cat/part woman," Eddie added.

They both turned to look at him. Richmond said:

"See Eddie is a writer. He knows this shit. We have to be somewhat esoteric." Diamond Jack said "Umm okey then," tilted his cap that looked like a train conductor's. He had no more to say on the subject, and prepared for a little snooze.

Cooper sipped at a bottle of schnapps, and plucked a miniature acoustic bass he carried for practice. He talked about his wife who had mental problems, but recently had some shock treatments and was improving. His job at the museum sounded mundane. When he spoke of it his eyes showed signs of a building madness that reminded Eddie why he avoided straight jobs. Cooper went off next about his asshole boss, most places had at least one, and that was another reason. They lunched on roast beef and cream cheese sandwiches that Richmond's considerate girlfriend had made and packed. Finally Seattle loomed ahead like a slightly different version of San Francisco. They found their way to the docks, down a service alley found the van and the second car. Equipment was being moved through an open back door. Eddie went over and carried some lighter items like cymbals, drum stool, a small extra amp and so on.

Backstage was a barren cold room that held a funky beat to hell couch and chair, along with a few other pieces of mismatched furniture. The room smelled of stale beer and cigarette smoke. Later the room became crowded with some of the local hipsters who were offering hits of coke, pot, booze. Eddie passed on everything, and instead asked a friendly guy who worked there where one might find a decent meal. Richmond joined Eddie for a meal. They came upon the amusement park-like atmosphere that surrounded the Space Needle. They went up it, then down it. They ate at what turned out to be a mediocre joint. But they had a good chat with a local musician they met there. Richmond offered to put him on the guest list: Mad Ox plus one. Mad Ox was built like a boxer, had a shaved head, biker tattoos, and spoke in a low timber voice. He was quite a likable and funny guy.

The hall was filled and the sound was superb. Eddie, feeling fresh after a shower and change of gear sat in the balcony with his feet up. A lot of dancing was happening near the stage. The light man was getting caught up in it all, doing some interesting maneuvers with his lights. Wolf Snake ended up doing two encores. Eddie saw that they were being filmed as well. The show was wildly successful. The after party strangely turned out to be a dud, or at least low key. Eddie had an interesting conversation with a blonde rocker chick with a sassy, inviting way about her, but all of a sudden it'd dawned on her that she had to get a ride home. He did get her number, but realized they were off for Portland in the morning.

In Portland they passed over a bridge. Below were a number

of bums and freight jumpers standing or sitting around. There were cardboard shacks, cooking fires, in fact a whole hobo encampment. One old guy waved at them with his wide brim hat. The sponsor lived outside the city in an impressive home in a wooded area. They were to relax, eat, use the pool, and enjoy themselves until their performance. It seemed to Eddie that in no time they were arriving to do the show. The small hall was in the basement of a building like a big log cabin. It turned out to have the worst acoustics imaginable. For some reason there had been no sound check, but it's highly doubtful it would have mattered much.

When Wolf Snake took the stage that was only one step up, it was apparent to Eddie that this was to be a disaster. And he was right: screeching feedback, instruments clashing, bass and drum like something you could drown in. Matt's voice lost in it all. Eddie could barely make out the songs through the noise. Some people held their ears and others just left. Some stood in awe, with open jaws as the band lumbered through the mind numbing metallic cacophony.

Finally, mercifully, it screeched to a stop; the band members looking at each other as if they had just survived a visit to hell, a manipulation of some prankster devil. There was weak applause, no encore and little talk while they loaded the van. Two youngsters with long hair wearing T-shirts with badly drawn skulls on them approached Diamond Jack and Richmond who were smoking cigarettes, and staring at nothing in particular. Eddie overheard the kids expressing their extreme appreciation for the performance. "I never heard anything like what you guys did tonight," one exclaimed wide-eyed. "Yeah man, that was so far out, like a metal army of Sun Ra or something," he looked at his friend to help explain. The other kid said: "Well, it's like you invented a new kind of music, noise music! When is your album coming out? We can't fucking wait!"

The drive was quiet. They arrived in Sacramento and pulled

into the lot of a motel that looked sleazy and corrupt. Once they checked in, their rooms became the play spaces for typical rock 'n roll behavior. First some local scensters showed up, some strippers, a couple of bikers, and other characters from the Delta who reminded Eddie of human lizards. Soon loud music blasted from different rooms: drugs, drink, sex, wild laughter, screaming, vomiting, and a fist fight, all occurring over the next few hours. Richmond had wisely locked up the room Eddie shared with him at the far end of the strip, but when Eddie went to it to use the bathroom, one of the bikers was standing near the entrance with his arms crossed smoking a devil headed pipe. He winked lewdly at Eddie. Eddie went in, and locked the door. What a freak show he thought. It kept up until the gig that evening in a bar down a back road with an audience of about twenty people and a sound system not a lot better than the last. Wolf Snake did a short set, stopping occasionally, to try to get it right, before finally giving up. They all looked drunk or half asleep to Eddie. He felt embarrassed for them. The audience dwindled down to a dozen, who didn't seem to give a damn either way, and looked to be much more interested in their own private affairs.

    The next day was completely different. Richmond called a meeting in the parking lot. He passed out joints, and gave a pep talk. He claimed that an evil earth spirit had descended on them in the Portland woods and had ignited a curse, but now it was gone, banished, due to a ritual he and a new friend, a local black guy, a "hoo doo man" named Chester had performed. Chester who stood nearby with a serious look dressed and looked like Arthur Lee of Love except he was darker, had a pot belly and wore multiple curious necklaces. After the talk the band did a sound check at a new place downtown that was a righteous hall like the place they played in Seattle. And that night they drew a healthy crowd and put on an outstanding show with a well balanced sound. Eddie, high on mushrooms and pot brownies found, himself in a good mood, dancing with a pretty red head by the stage. Wolf Snake had recouped, recovered and delivered the goods. They could now return to San Francisco feeling like they had lost some battles, but ultimately had won the war.

Eddie had found the experience of traveling with a band interesting, but probably not something he wanted to do much more. And that feeling extended to the Wolf Snake scene in general. Eddie would stay in touch and visit again and definitely check out a show some night, but he didn't want to be part of the inner circle. He was more interested in Dr. Kublar, what he could learn, how he could be transformed, and how he could become a real writer. It felt good to finally rest his head on the pillow in his own bed, nestled away in Chinatown which is always more mysterious and enchanting in the evening.

8

A few nights later Eddie joined Dr. Kublar on the roof. They reclined on striped deck chairs that Mu brought out. There were some potted plants, and a clothes line with only a couple of silk handkerchiefs fluttering in the breeze. The pagoda roof behind Dr. Kublar was lit by the setting sun. The skyline was magnificent. Electric reds, and oranges streaking the sky created a dramatic vignette for Eddie, who'd been seriously thinking of getting back to writing. He always liked to begin with a description. Dr. Kublar was dressed in a cloak that's neck and button line were covered in small, bone colored sea shells. Eddie would learn the cloak had been designed by the doctor, but assembled by Peruvian tribeswomen. The brown leather collar was high, and rounded off or molded, and marked with what looked to be ancient symbols. The doctor was wearing his small black sunglasses. Eddie was pleasantly surprised to see Mu pushing a tray on wheels over to them, parking it in-between them. On it were two large bamboo pipes with small bowls.

"Edward, what if I said that the marijuana we are going to smoke is from an ancient time, a lost world? That it has been preserved by a select group down through the ages? And that smoking it is like no other psychedelic experience you've ever had?"

Eddie looked at Mu who was arranging kitchen matches in a small wooden saucer. "I'd say wow." Mu gave him his cat smile and handed Eddie a pipe. Eddie put it to his lips. Mu lit a match, delicately placing it in the air at a precise spot. Eddie drew, and as the smoke filled his lungs he was transported to a very different place:

...a backward voice...I begin to decipher a voice line. Or? I take another hit at Mu's urging...looking at Dr. Kublar who is glowing, levitating...entering a curious world of Indian deities, depicted in gaudy, spiritual paintings: something like the cover for that Hendrix album: "Axis Bold as Love"...blue skin, pink leggings, red lips, golden crowns and each holding a large pink sacred lotus...all floating by...eyeballs of all sizes zooming in from each direction stopping on a dime from some distant place...even larger ones floating down, down from the sky...looking at me looking at them looking at me...as they rolled away, becoming smaller...smaller...I am walking with Dr. Kublar off of the rooftop that has turned to ice?...to a road I had glimpsed before...drastic shift—we're in a carriage of sorts, traveling at an incredible speed...the passing scenery of shooting stars, some exploding... psychedelic fireworks...Then slo mo...an unknown creature from some other time, or world floating next to us...thinking of the fairy tales...as a child: a triangular head, deep set yellow eyes...sharp nose...slit mouth, its skin gray, smooth, with short arms and legs, whispers of a long tail. It does summersaults there in the space... locking eyes with Dr. Kublar before everything shatters into golden specs falling....I feel as though tumbling down a black tunnel....

Eddie opened his eyes and found everything back to normal. Dr. Kublar sipped tea.

"That was amazing," said Eddie. They remained in silence resting there for some time.

Dr. Kublar began to speak at length about his plan to guide Eddie through a noble transformation, beginning with the return of the heist money.

"I'm concerned about finances though," Eddie said. "How

will I pay the rent, eat? I must find employment first, don't you think?" he asked in a drowsy voice.

"No, not at all, and for your transformation the sooner the money is returned the better. That is your negative voice speaking now. The one that does not have your best interest at heart. It's quite the opposite in fact, a parasite really, or a vampire as I prefer. I tell you money and means will not be a worry, and of little concern on your new path."

Eddie did believe what he said was true. That helped dampen his fear which was really fear of the unknown. And so he made arrangements the following day to wrap up the remaining money and mail it back to the restaurant owner. The balance from Eddie's end would be sent in payments at later dates. He included an anonymous note explaining that he would send additional payments until his half of the funds had been returned. He left the door open, and began doing his weekly cleaning of the apartment. He left the window open as well, and it created a draft that suddenly stopped. He turned to find Dr. Kublar standing in the doorway, dressed in a black three piece suit, a purple shirt, and a purple flowery tie.

"Off to deal with some bureaucratic nonsense that requires this attire, although I do despise the whole charade. But, there's no way to avoid it in this so-called free country."

Eddie had a rag in his hand, and was wearing pajama bottoms, and a Wolf Snake T-shirt that was too big.

"You've done a nice job with this room." His eyes fell across the head on the dresser that Eddie had purchased at the herb shop.

"May I?" Dr. Kublar asked, approaching it.

Eddie sat on the bed, and saw that a toenail trimming was in order.

Dr. Kublar examined the curious head closely.

"How did you come by this Edward?"

Eddie told him the story while finding his bedroom slippers, and stepping into them. Dr. Kublar continued to examine the head.

"Edward I believe this might be a valuable artifact. I would like to borrow it, and have an expert take a look. If I'm right you should have no more money concerns."

"Really? The man I bought it from said it was fake." Eddie wondered if in fact his luck was already changing.

When Eddie came back from breakfast he found something new and wonderful in his room. A small desk had been placed in a corner with a chair, and a Remington manual typewriter that although old, looked to be in fine condition. Eddie had told the doctor that he was thinking of returning to fiction writing, something he felt he had an affinity for, but had fallen out of practice. Eddie had always written by hand, mostly by printing, so he could better decipher what it was that he'd written. He did however know how to type. During his time in Catholic school he'd signed up for the typing class because it was the only class that was coed. A friend had hipped him to that, although when he'd shown up for class he found a pretty yet stern nun who watched constantly for wandering eyes.

She had caught Eddie peeping at a girl's legs, and smacked his fingers with a ruler right away. Eddie endured a couple more swats that the nun obviously enjoyed handing out before he buckled down, learned the home keys, and learned how to type. He then became the star pupil. This gave him some leeway from the nun, a quick smile instead of a brisk whack for stolen eye contact with one of the girls.

So now he sat down, inserted some paper, and fired away, familiarizing himself with the keyboard again. Then something took over. His fingers began to pick out the keys at a lightening speed, as a story began to unfold in his head. He was translating from another force, another source. He stopped, at first startled by the sensation, similar to what he'd felt at the Wizard Stones. He dove back in, and an hour later stopped, looked at the gathered pages before him. Most of it made sense: a couple is running from the police; after some close calls they make it out of the country to Switzerland. The man begins waking up at night with a strange voice speaking in his head. He writes down the messages. They seem to have their own logic. He becomes obsessed with their meaning. One day a government official shows up to take a survey. The man finds the official suspicious since some of the questions repeat the cryptic messages he'd received. Eddie put the pages aside. He would look at them closer later in the evening. He would mark them up, and make some notes on where they could possibly lead.

The following day Mu tapped lightly on his door, and announced that the doctor had invited him to lunch. Eddie was about to make a sandwich, but said sure, since the doctor's meals were always wonderful. It also gave him another opportunity to hear this most interesting man speak, and think out loud. Eddie followed Mu to the apartment. He was led into yet another room he hadn't been to: a nook of sorts, with a skylight. It had a booth like a diner. The doctor was already seated drinking a glass of water. Eddie said hello, and thanked him for the invite. The doctor was wearing a blue silk robe with sleeves that flowed out widely at the lower arms. He was not wearing sunglasses, although it was rather bright in the room from the skylight. His eyes were gray, and deep. Eddie felt they held a strong magnetism. Dr. Kublar was served the same biscuit as always. Eddie was served a bowl of mildly spicy lentil soup with slices of avocado on top from a Tunisian recipe. A brown bread was served with a glass of carrot juice. The doctor encouraged Eddie to eat and he did, thoroughly enjoying it.

"A distinguished, and brilliant scholar from Peking is arriving here tomorrow. He will be studying your ten dollar head along with a local expert in Chinese historical artifacts. Until then it remains under lock and key by a trusted associate, but I have a good feeling about its worth."

"That would be extraordinary news for sure. By the way doctor, this soup is delicious. Mu is a master chef eh?"

"Yes, he is many things. I'm glad you find it satisfactory. Nutrition is one of the principles that must be studied, understood and practiced. Know how to evaluate nutrient density in food."

"But I never see you eat anything other than that biscuit."

"Ah but Edward, it is not just any biscuit. One day you'll have one as well, but not yet. I'll tell you this, there will come a time that nutrient seekers will make themselves known, and after years of study, and development they will discover (due to a shrinking food supply) how to make something like this biscuit and refer to themselves as the biscuit people. I do partake in jook on occasion. It must be prepared correctly, though, and topped with only ginger and scallion. You are invited the next time we have it, but it must eaten very early. Daybreak is best."

Eddie finished the soup, and used the remaining bread to wipe his bowl clean. He drank the rest of the juice. Mu cleared the table. Doctor Kublar pulled a cigarette case from an inner pocket, flipped it open, offered Eddie one. Eddie shook his head, but the doctor insisted.

"This is not tobacco Edward, it is made entirely from herbs. It is good for you in fact."

So Eddie took one, and accepted a light from Mu who was back at his side with one of his kitchen matches. The doctor lit his own with a thin silver lighter he looked to have snatched out of the air. Eddie drew on the cigarette and tasted something wonderful: an aroma more fragrant than the finest cigar, like something gathered from a magical garden, something the caterpillar might have smoked in Alice. The doctor smiled with his eyes seeing how Eddie enjoyed it.

"Now that is something," Eddie commented. "And that pot

we smoked on the roof! I'm still thinking about, better than any acid trip I've ever had, yet short in duration, which is a plus. And there were no after effects, no coming down feeling. A beautiful thing. How did you acquire it?"

"Edward I am now recording my life adventures, my travels, awakenings, experiences, wisdom gained, lessons learned, and trials and tribulations as the intense yet misguided brethren of this country sometimes say. That ancient marijuana was from Atlantis, or the original Lemuria. How I came by that sealed vase is a fantastic story that I've only just revealed to Mu for the autobiography. I can share an edited version if you like."

"Excellent," Eddie said. "I do appreciate it, and by the way I want to thank you for the typewriter. I tried it out and found it much to my liking."

"Good, I thought you might. It was collecting dust up here. It belonged to a crime writer who mysteriously disappeared in Chinatown, I was told. Mu records everything on tape, and keeps short hand notes, he then transcribes everything on an electric, and presents me with pages that I must then edit, again and again and again. Mu likes the hum of an electric typewriter. He says it soothes him as he works."

Mu filled the doctor's glass with Moroccan mint tea and poured one for Eddie as well.

9

"Of all places to receive such a gift it occurred in Mexico City, D.F.," Dr. Kublar said. "I was recovering from a most strenuous jungle excursion to study a new Mayan ruin that had been recently uncovered. I had picked up some exotic infection that was keeping me in bed. My contact in the capitol, a well studied occultist himself, recommended I see a special doctor, not an MD but a brujo, a spirit man who had moved to the capitol to dispel a curse that a sorcerer adversary had placed on him.

"I took a taxi out to a barrio that appeared more dangerous than the jungle I had been been recently traversing. I was still sweating and wracked with spasms that left me light headed. Once we entered that neighborhood the taxi driver made the sign of the cross. That gave me pause since he had come across as a rather fearless and robust individual. He thanked Jesus out loud when he spotted a man waiting and waving at the address of our destination. The man directed the cab into an open garage attached to the building. The driver was taken to the kitchen by a maid for refreshments. I was taken up a small caged elevator to the top floor by the garage man. I was directed into a large room filled with bookcases, fantastic paintings, massive, curious tree sculptures, and left alone. At least I thought I was alone; the brujo emerged from a dark corner to greet me with bright eyes. He clasped both of my hands.

"You've come! You've finally come!" He directed me to a

comfortable chair. He was in his fifties I would say, short, and on the lean side. He wore a gray hooded poncho, black, loosely fitting pants, and nearly destroyed huraches. He had a clean shaven face, a pleasant demeanor and thanked me again for coming. I didn't catch on at first, thinking perhaps that he was simply dying for company. I told him my symptoms. He looked in my eyes and my mouth with a magnifying glass and felt my pulse. He left the room, and came back with a black box that he sat on a table that looked like his work bench. He began to make a mixture from bottles and containers that were there. At one point the mixture smoked, but finally settled into a liquid that was thick and dark yellow. I was afraid this was my medicine. It was, and at his insistence I drank it all. It tasted like the essence of an alien and fantastic planet unknown to earth men.

"The brujo invited me to join him at the table. He rolled out an old scroll map, weighing down the ends with beakers, a coffee mug, and an ashtray, which I remember advertised the pyramids of the sun and the moon. The map was of ancient worlds. He pointed out different peculiar symbols. "Look, there! The signs of the ancient ones!"

"He rolled it up again and asked how I was feeling. I felt perfectly well I told him; the symptoms were completely gone. He gave me one more dose to take first thing in the morning. And then he asked me to sit down again.

"The brujo lifted the black shiny box above him. He closed his eyes and muttered something under his breath. He placed the box back on the table. He opened it and the room went dark, although a dim glow lit his face like when as a kid you turn a flashlight on at your chin in the dark to evoke a spooky mood. But this glow was golden, so golden and magnificent you felt you could touch it. He extracted something else from the box, and closed it. His head sagged as if he was suddenly exhausted. The light gradually returned to the room. Rejuvenated the brujo raised his head, and was back to his old self. He held a black container the size of an ink well out to me.

"Dr. Kublar, you were directed to me. You need to know no more. You see I have cured you. The box I have just opened contains magic from lost and ancient worlds. Each item has a home with a trusted protector, and one who will use it wisely. This container holds what is left of the sacred herb that was smoked by the ancient ones. It's what's called pot or marijuana today, but this my friend is a hundred times more powerful, and is self replenishing. As long as a portion is kept in this container it will re-grow itself."

He must have sensed Eddie's doubt since he said next that they should celebrate with a smoke. "I had smoked from time to time in my travels, and as you've learned partaken in opium and sampled other drugs, but always wisely, cautiously, reading about the effects, advantages and disadvantages, speaking with experts beforehand. The brujo came up with a bamboo pipe like the ones we used the other day. With tweezers he placed some of the ancient drug into the bowl. It reminded me of kif smoking in North Africa except the pipe was thick, and the bowl was shaped in a triangle. I drew on the pipe as the brujo waved a match rather high over the bowl, and muttered bueno, bueno, muy bueno.

"My experience was probably something like your own: surreal landscapes, an out of body experience, new psychic terrain and convoluted space as seen though the eyes of a mad psychedelic seer, or combinations thereof. The brujo instructed me to smoke at a certain time on a weekly basis, and I would find a portal that would open, and through it I would be able to visit the ancient worlds, albeit briefly. I would also need a Dialer; more about that later.

"Worlds Edward that are beyond our imagination, more akin to our dream world that at times is so real you feel you might disappear into it. Over the years I have learned how to make the experience last longer, and be more fruitful. Only recently I have been able to speak with one of the ancients during a visit. Alas, I can tell you no more for now, nor may I include these conversations in my book as of yet. I'm only allowed to say what I've said. You must adhere to ancient laws and special procedures."

Eddie was on his way out the following morning when Mu appeared from around a corner, startling him. He was holding some clothing in front of him and offered the bundle to Eddie.

"What is it Mu? What is this?"

"The doctor would like you to wear prease. And come to apartment for instructions."

Eddie, a little reluctantly took the clothes which turned out to be sweat pants, and sweat shirt, gray in color, and fresh smelling. Eddie looked at his watch. He had no definite plans, a walk maybe, have a coffee, and read the paper. He wasn't really in the mood for a workout. Dr. Kublar certainly had some kind of exercise instructions in mind. Eddie wasn't crazy about the idea. He never had been, although he'd been a ball player as a kid. He even made a team, and was carried on the backs of his teammate's after pitching a no-hitter to win the little league championship. And he was a swimmer. He had become a lifeguard and saved two children's lives one summer, the first in a quarry in rural Pennsylvania, the other at a pool where he worked. But exercise class in gym? Like many others, he found unpleasant and generally skipped it, like many of his other classes. In fact he was mostly skipping school, especially in the spring so he could laze away the day in a park with a good book, or take a lunch to the swimming hole, or hang out in one of the pool halls he loved. Self education, but that's how he started getting in trouble. They called it truancy.

Mu was waiting for an answer as Eddie's gym clothes inspired reminiscing having ended. "Okay Mu, tell the doctor I'll be up shortly." He put on the clothes, which fit perfectly, and laced his Converse low-cuts.

At the apartment Mu led him up a metal stairway to the rooftop. There he found Dr. Kublar dressed in identical gear already warming up, swinging his arms to and fro. He instructed Eddie to stand next to him and copy his movements. Eddie had seen others practicing this Tai Chi exercise in the parks in small groups, always Chinese, but once he did see a hippie couple join a group of older Chinese women. Eddie copied the doctor's poses and moves. They faced west, and a reluctant sun fell in and out of view because of the fog. They faced east, north and south. The air was crisp yet Eddie almost at once felt the chill he had been experiencing earlier dissipate.

Eddie followed the doctor through a serious of different exercises, some quite curious. Eddie laughed once, but cut it off after a stern look from the doctor. He followed Dr. Kublar over to a pole, imitated what he called the ape swing. "You will never have back problems," Dr. Kublar said, "...like most western males, if you do this every other day." Next they did something called the human clock, positioning themselves against the wall to a shed, making their arms perform like the hands on a clock. They held imaginary large balls, and did a number of strange facial exercises. On their knees they bowed to the sun, and then did twenty regular gym-style pushups. Standing up again, Dr. Kublar instructed him on a warrior's stance, and a combination of combative maneuvers and tricks. Eddie loathed violence and did his best to avoid it, although growing up he had to defend himself against bullies a few times—twice he had come out on top, and once had taken a beating, but the bully didn't go away unmarked either. Dr. Kublar had him attack him and easily had Eddie on the mat each time. The last time the doctor did something with his left hand, moving it fluidly in the air in a way Eddie could swear the doctor had conjured up an actual bird. He was so mesmerized the doctor quickly knocked his legs out from under him.

On their backs now, they did a number of leg exercises, then in a seated yoga posture a series of breathing exercises that eventually gave Eddie a floating sensation. Dr. Kublar had him focus on a simple non-exerting four count of breath. Soon Eddie felt grounded again. The doctor stood effortlessly and offered him a hand. Eddie took a seat and watched as the doctor opened a black case presented by Mu. The doctor turned and was now rotating three large silver balls in each hand, then counter clockwise, and then they moved in a whirl, and he was juggling them too. After Eddie said wow and far out the doctor turned and replaced the balls in the case Mu had continued to hold.

"I'll teach you the iron ball mediation one day. You'll start with two balls," he said, laughed, but quickly with a serious look, added, "A most ancient practice Edward. This was an outstanding first day, and if you agree to join me we'll do this twice a week. I do it anyhow everyday. Don't answer yet. See how you feel as you go through the day, and how you sleep tonight."

Eddie agreed, thanked him for the instructions, and returned to his apartment for a shower. He changed back into street clothes, and headed out. But now he felt an extra spring in his step, more energy that he'd experienced in some time. The exercise routine? It must be, he thought, but wondered if there would be a crash. He walked downtown and after soaking up the sun for a while in Union Square Park he visited his favorite record store. He bought albums by two artists that the British rock press had been saying were the latest sensation, the spokesmen for Glam Rock: Marc Bolan and David Bowie. It was said that these two artists were a radical yet logical extension of Mod, which was how Eddie often identified himself, both music-wise and style-wise. He sometimes wondered if he wouldn't have fit in better in London or New York than San Francisco, although, considering his relationship and experiences with Dr. Kublar he realized he was in exactly the right place, at exactly the right time.

As he was leaving the record store he ran into Richmond, who was accompanied by a striking black girl sporting a dyed platinum buzz cut.

"Eddie my man, where have you been keeping yourself?" he said, sounding a bit black himself. "This is Connie, my new best friend, and honey this is Eddie, also from the burg, and a cat who knows a lot about music."

"Is that right," said Connie. "Let me test you. Who played with Curtis Knight and the Squires before starting a solo career?"

"Jimi Hendrix born 1946 as Johnny Allen Hendrix."

"Not bad. Okay who originally sang Hound Dog?"

"Big Mama Thorton."

"Gosh you are good. Okay one more — who did Funky Broadway?"

"That would be Dyke and the Blazers in 1966."

"Okay, I'm thoroughly impressed. What did you just buy Ed?" He showed her the Electric Warrior, and Ziggy Stardust albums. He saw that neither of them had a clue. Richmond asked:

"Yeah? This stuff is good? Never heard of either one."

"Oh you will, especially Bowie. He's gone beyond the whole Rolling Stones and Velvet Underground thing." Eddie said, repeating what he'd read in the British rock magazine. "London is going bananas over him. T. Rex front man Marc Bolan actually led the way attracting a lot of teeny boppers."

Richmond was studying the record jackets closely, said maybe he should give them a listen since Wolf Snake had landed a record deal and would begin recording in one week.

"Congratulations! How exciting for you." Eddie gave Richmond a biker hug and a soft punch on the shoulder.

"I thought I'd pick up some new sounds since I've only been listening to our demos day and night. What else do you recommend?"

"Well, this record by Roxy Music is supposed to be good as

well. And, let's see you can't go wrong with the MC5, in fact they're something like you guys."

"I know the MC5 motherfucker."

They all shared a laugh.

Richmond looked over the records that Eddie suggested while Connie flipped through the rhythm and blues section. Eddie joined her, showed her a new album by Ike Turner, and pointed out that a Sam and Dave tune was playing on the store's sound system. It turned out she knew the song too, and together they began singing along, grooving. The Chinese clerk, who was sporting a huge fro, was smiling. Afterward they went out for pizza at a place where you had to stand. They had slices, and cokes. Richmond mentioned that Alice had been asking about him, and that got a look from Connie. Eddie said that he'd been busy writing again and hoped to complete a novel. Connie showed interest in that too, and started to talk about books and writers. She was again impressed that Eddie had read black writers like Donald Goines, Iceberg Slim and Chester Himes.

"So what's your stuff like?"

"Oh, maybe Jack Kerouac meets Ian Fleming meets Lewis Carroll."

"Wow," she said and Richmond didn't look particularly pleased that she'd taken such a shine to Eddie. He switched topics back to the recording session. Richmond asked Eddie if he would like to be one of the select few to sit in on the sessions. Eddie said he would be honored and thanked him. Richmond gave him the address, time and place and a secret code word to get in.

10

When Eddie arrived back in Chinatown he was anxious to hear the records he'd purchased. He dimmed the lights the way he liked it, hit a water pipe, and put the T. Rex album on. At first he wasn't quite sure since the voice was strange, like a elf character from a demented fairy tale. The lyrics were certainly trippy. The music itself had a different sound and groove than he was used to. Eddie knew that some music had to have repeated listening, and that would certainly hold true for something different, something that didn't follow the same mold, the usual form. And as he listened something clicked. He became aware that he had indeed taken a step in his listening scope, then in another moment it all made sense. By the second spin of the record, he was a convert. It was addicting. A munchie attack came over him. He took a break to eat a some fortune cookies, and brew a cup of tea. He reloaded his water pipe, and took a deep hit. If Bolan took him to the moon, Ziggy Stardust sent him all the way to Mars. It made the Mod scene that Eddie embraced seem almost passé. It was a brave new world, and Eddie decided that he would step into it more, and glam up his looks. The next day he went back to the store, bought an older Bowie record, the Roxy Music album, and a rare Jerry Lee Lewis live recording. He also bought some blue eye shadow at Woolworth's, two shirts at a sale at Macy's, one, chartreuse with sparkled gold on the cuffs, collar and button placket, the other bright blue, sparkled silver the same way. Damn they're glam he thought.

Eddie's writing continued with a three hour session each morning on the old Remington. A voice spoke in his head as he was transcribing. Later in the evening he would read the pages over, mark them up. One evening while he was looking over his pages Mu tapped on his door.

"Doctor Kublar would be verly preased for you to join in morning for joke."

"I'm sorry Mu, but what? To tell me a joke?"

"Prease read Mr. Edward," Mu said handing him a paper. "... and if you care to join be ready by 7 AM. Good evening Mr. Edward."

Eddie dropped back on his bed, and under his reading lamp read an article about jook, pronounced: joke. It was basically rice soup, served as a breakfast food, often referred to as congree, or porridge. One could order a variety of different meats like duck, pork, fish or eggs to be included within. It was sprinkled with ginger, and onion. Sometimes a drop of soy sauce was added. It was often served with a fried donut like bread, and rice noodles dipped in soy sauce. Eddie remembered it was the one dish that Dr. Kublar said he would go out on rare occasions to have. 7 AM was early to be up and going out to eat, but Eddie had decided that regarding Dr. Kublar, he was along for the ride wherever that may lead. His experiences so far had been thrilling, adventurous and mind expanding.

At 7 AM Eddie was dressed. He'd decided to try out his new look on the doctor and Mu. He was wearing the silver sparkle shirt with a black velvet jacket, a touch of blue eye shadow. He slicked his shag behind his ears. He was singing the tune "Suffragette City" as he looked in the mirror. He opened his door to find Dr. Kublar and Mu. The doctor was wearing a long coat that reminded Eddie of the Edwardian period. Mu was wearing a track suit, with his pigtail trailing under a long billed hat like a duck hunter might wear. The doctor greeted him without the slightest comment or hint of surprise at Eddie glamming it up. They walked through the alleyways of Chinatown, Mu ahead of them, then behind, then to both sides, always changing, alert, watching for any sign of danger: Assassins is what Eddie thought as he noted Mu's stealthy, fluid movements and darting eyes. The doctor paid no mind at all. Under a street lamp shaped like a lantern they passed a pile of wooden crates stacked haphazardly with ginseng peeking out.

Guided by Mu now, they went down a hidden walkway off a dark alley, through a door and then through a series of tarps onto an elevator. They descended, and emerged in an underground city that mimicked Chinatown above. Everywhere were wonders for Eddie's eyes: open gambling clubs, whore houses with the ladies in windows posing, on balconies, opium dens with the fumes drifting onto the street, shoe shine and newspaper stands, curio shops, Chinese men smoking bamboo pipes in cafés, and more alleyways leading to yet more of the same. Heading down a long wood paneled hallway they came to the "The kitchens of Jook" as the doctor called them. A long line of enormous vats of the thick rice soup were being stirred by stoic Chinese men. Dr. Kublar directed Eddie to a back booth while Mu went ahead and placed the orders.

"I've heard stories about a secret underground city beneath Chinatown but figured it was a myth based on some of the actual underground opium dens in the 1800s or early 1900 in Seattle."

"Yes, and that is what everybody thinks, and that is why it remains in existence. Since you are with us you are a trusted lo fawn, a white ghost you are permitted to see and experience what few others ever will."

Mu joined them. He sat next to the doctor, pouring tea for three that was delivered by a young girl who exchanged some remarks with Mu as dishes being cleared clacked noisily in the background. The doctor laughed.

"She said she finds you cute, and like someone who stepped out of a fable," Dr. Kublar said.

The jook arrived: three bowls of plain porridge garnished with thin strips of ginger and bits of scallion. Eddie followed the doctor and added a nip of soy sauce. The girl next served them a huge plate of fried bread pieces that were to be dipped into the rice soup. Then she brought them individual plates of thick rice noodles in soy sauce. Eddie knew how to use chop sticks by now. They all dug in with soup spoons and devoured the fare. Afterward they dabbed their lips with napkins, and sipped jasmine tea.

"That was wonderful," said Eddie, "...and this whole experience is mind blowing."

"Now we will visit an old friend of mine," said Dr. Kublar.

As they left the waitresses whispered, and smiled. Eddie wondered if he would be allowed to return, or could even find the place on his own. After traversing a conundrum of alleyways, passing through multiple secret doorways, walking down a winding stairway, deeper underground, and finally taking a rickshaw to an alleyway where the shop's windows sparkled and glistened with gold, jewels, and extravagant porcelain vases. At the end of the short alley they went into a shop that looked to specialize in Chinese antiquities. A boy who looked and dressed the way Mu did at the apartment escorted them through a velvet curtain to a lavish back room whose opulence rivaled that of Dr. Kublar's sitting room.

The boy directed them to chairs facing a pedestal on which something was draped with a piece of white silk. A man came out of a back room and to Eddie's surprise was a Caucasian, older, good looking gentleman maybe in his seventies. He was trim, fit, and sporting a white pencil mustache. His hair receded in such a devilish way it made him even more handsome. He wore a dark suit, white shirt, and a striped tie. He waved his hand and asked everyone to stay seated, although Dr. Kublar didn't looked like he was about to rise. The man greeted the doctor with a two handed handshake, Mu a regular one. Then he approached Eddie who was sitting on the doctor's left hand side.

"And this is the lucky young man," he said offering his boney hand, insisting again that Eddie stay seated, and palming him a glitzy red and gold packet. He spoke in a whispery voice.

"That is lucky candy. Enjoy. My name is Mr. Garret, and this is my shop Edward. You may call me Phillip. I have done business with collectors from all over the world. I've had treasures that you would not believe pass through here. The doctor and I have been close friends for over thirty years. We've seen much together. You would not have connected with this man in the way you have except for powers and sources greater than our own at work. We are all recipients of the guardians. And now you have come across a treasure that will certainly put whatever concerns you have for financial security to rest. That you discovered this near the doctor's private residence, and bought it from someone whom I've since investigated and found is a servant for a sinister organization who would do harm to the recipients if ordered to, is equally astounding. But the man like many of our enemies, is blinded by hate and arrogance.

"Now Edward, let me tell you what you have acquired, purchased and legally own."

Mr. Garret pulled the silk covering off the head that Eddie had bought for ten dollars. It really was a bit gruesome with its large forehead, bulging, malevolent eyes, mean meager mouth, deep cheek lines, and ears shaped like big question marks.

Mr. Garret's clear blue eyes seemed to gleam as he stared at the head.

"Edward there are only a handful of these thought to exist. It is sandstone and heavy as you know, around fifty pounds. But did you know it is a Lohan sculpture from the Tang Dynasty, over

1,000 years old? It was made during a time when poetry, art and science intertwined. My theory is they were created to ward off evil.

"I have an interested buyer, a private collector in Connecticut who will pay a high price once the proper paperwork is done. When all is said and done your end of the deal will be 500 thousand dollars. The doctor and myself will take finder, authentication and negotiating fees. There are lawyer fees to insure all taxes have been paid, and paperwork is ship shape. Two hundred thousand does all that, and a remaining fifty thousand I suggest we donate to a charity that we can all agree on. Now you Edward Knox, you must state that you purchased the head at a flea market, a silly but necessary white lie. We'll give you the details, school you in fact to make this narrative and hence deal itself solid and airtight. So, Edward, what do you say?"

"I'm flabbergasted. Who'd have thought?" The almost incomprehensible amount of money was whizzing through Eddie's brain but strangely he was not thinking about spending it, but rather about investing it securely and letting it grow. These men, Eddie thought would show him how to invest.

"Dr. Kublar," Mr. Garret said. gesturing respectfully, "....likely saved it from indeed ending up in a flea market one day which is the same to my mind as collecting dust in the corner of an herb shop."

Eddie stood and stepped closer to the head. He studied it with his hands behind his back as if he was in a museum. Even before he knew what it was he'd felt that it was a deep, mysterious thing made by a wild, creative person, someone who had experienced and understood darkness. Eddie marveled at its age, breathtaking in its magnitude....

11

When Richmond told Eddie by phone that the recording session's location had been moved to LA, he added that the offer for him to join them, was still open even for the whole week if he liked. He sounded pleasantly surprised by Eddie's answer.

"Out of sight! That's even better. I've never been to LA and I've always wanted to visit."

"Excellent Eddie, but the cost would be yours, you know?"

"Not a problem. This is really exciting. To be part of rock 'n roll history and all," Eddie added to further please Richmond.

"Yeah man, Wolf Snake's first album. It will change the fucking world, well at least the world of music."

Eddie arranged to meet him the following day at a downtown travel agency to purchase plane tickets. He figured he would go to the band's hotel, check the rates, and if they weren't too bad stay there himself. The record label was fronting the bill for the band, but the budget was tight. They had a minder assigned to keep tabs on the costs. Eddie told Dr. Kublar about the trip. He asked Eddie to do him a favor while in LA: deliver a letter that he had planned to send through the post, but much preferred the personal approach of a messenger, like in days of old. Eddie gladly agreed. Dr. Kublar had changed the course of his life he felt and was guiding him toward some transformation, toward a connection with his guardian.

The flight to LA was uneventful. Eddie was surprised at how

short it was. Before he knew it they were piling into a rented van and barreling down a freeway, then cruising Sunset Strip. There was a feeling in the air that was not in San Francisco Eddie decided, a torrid, steamy feel. But he sensed a doomed future for the city where everyone would be forced live in bubble homes elevated above a encroaching boiling sea sealed off against poisonous mists. Eddie was imagining this, and considering writing a science fiction story set in a futuristic LA. After some looking around he found a motel not far from the band's: friendlier and nearly half the price. He arranged rental of a car through the hotel to secure his independence.

Eddie was working on his story idea in a notebook in his room overlooking a medium size pool when a couple of shapely, tanned girls showed up. They slipped off white robes and prepared to sunbathe. They each wore silver mylar bikinis. Eddie found it impossible to keep his mind on the developing story. He decided to go for a swim and possibly meet them. He changed, and gathered his gear, including a copy of The Dice Man that he was halfway through. He didn't set up too far away from them. But when he passed them, he thought they might be a tad on the young side. He decided to enjoy a swim, and get some sun instead of trying to chat. The water was cool when he dove in from one side of the pool, though it was refreshing and invigorating too. Eddie was a good swimmer and proceeded to swim from one end to the other in various styles. As he switched to a backstroke he felt someone beside him. It was the blonde. She was smiling and looked like a million bucks to him. She seemed older than he thought previously. He stopped and treaded water.

"Hi I'm Melanie. You're a good swimmer."

"Oh, just alright I guess. I'm Eddie." They shook wet hands. "I just arrived this afternoon from San Francisco. Where are you two from?"

"We're from right here Eddie. We're crashing this pool. We

pick a different one every day, although we have some favorites. At some the staff even know us, like here, so it's no problem." Melanie gave him another smile, and looked over to the dark haired one who was sitting up now. She had star shaped white frame sunglasses propped on her head so she could better examine her toenails.

"Come and join us, Urs!" Melanie called out. Eddie wondered if maybe Urs was Eastern European, but he would learn it was short for Ursula. Urs climbed the steps to the diving board, executed a perfect jack knife, and moments later popped up in between them. She was equally as pretty. Eddie would learn that they were cousins, who worked as instructors at a private health spa in Hollywood. Eddie told them what had brought him to LA. They were intrigued although neither had heard of Wolf Snake. They knew all about David Bowie, Alice Cooper, T. Rex and Roxy Music though, and began singing different tunes they had memorized.

Urs looked at Eddie's book when they climbed out of the pool and were drying off. She said she'd heard it was good. Eddie said it was fascinating, and inspiring his own work.

"So Eddie," Melanie said. "Are you going to invite us to your room for a drink?" Eddie made a sweeping gesture, bowed, said:

"Goddesses of the pool: you are hereby invited to my humble resting lodge, a place that could never be worthy of your royalty but perhaps you would bless it with your presence."

They laughed, and Melanie said: "He's a writer all right." They took an elevator to his floor.

Inside the room things happened so fast Eddie barely had time to think. The mini-bar was opened, cocktails were made, drank, and made again. A joint came from somewhere, along with black beauties from Urs. The girls undressed, dried off, and danced. They bounced around provoking each other on the bed, feeling good. Urs found a radio station she liked. Melanie jabbed at him, and teased him about his white skin. On the second drink he found himself wrestling a little, clowning around, then being naked and attended to in a way he'd never experienced before, never having been with two girls at once. These two knew exactly what they were doing, and were not shy about it. After the play period where Urse finally brought him to orgasm, they put on the Glam street gear that they had in beach bags. Eddie sat up in bed with wonder plastered all over his face. He watched them fawning in the mirror. Melanie wrote down her number on the motel's note pad, and said to call if the band had any parties. They kissed him goodbye, said they'd had fun, and hoped to see him later. Eddie, drained, rolled over, and rested, but could not sleep.

Eddie took a walk around the neighborhood at sunset, and thought he would have a meal. He was still reliving the menage a trois in his head, and coming off the speed, still a bit aroused. He soon realized that Hollywood was not much of a walking around place. There were areas, neighborhoods one could walk, but a car was essential. Before long he was driving down Sunset Boulevard toward Venice Beach, one of the places he'd noted that he wanted to visit.

He found parking near the beach. He liked the place, obviously a more hipster, independently minded neighborhood. The Beats had had a scene here, he remembered from his reading. He settled for an Italian restaurant off the beach, and had a plate of pasta, salad, a glass of the house Chianti. The meal was as good as any he'd had in North Beach in San Francisco. Satisfied he walked back to the beach, smoked part of a joint there. He walked along looking out at the ocean, caught up in a myriad of thoughts: reliving experiences, thinking about Dr. Kublar, considering that now he had no money worries, that he was alive, that he had a book to write, and that he had an entrance into a secret world, one entrenched with magic.

He spotted Santa Monica Pier, and turned inland to get up

onto it. At the end, next to a hot dog and soft pretzel stand he saw a sign for a fortune teller. He thought it would be a lark. He found he was fairly high when he walked into the small room done up with mirrors, candles, and curious objects. He heard what he thought at first was an eerie soundtrack, but then realized it was the wind that had kicked up outside. The fortune teller was a old woman, who made him think of a crone from some ancient fable. She wore layers of ethnic garb and countless necklaces and bracelets and moved around the room with the quickness of a child. She sat across from him. He could feel her presence, a definite magnetic pull. She rolled out a piece of material that turned out to be the scaly skin of some reptile. She took his hand, and began to speak in an cracking voice that would at times rise higher in pitch. He was taken aback a bit by it all. The lark had become something else, and his thoughts had turned serious. He knew he would engage with this woman the best he could.

 Eddie left the fortune teller's certain that he'd connected to the spirit world, and was only now stepping back into reality. The old lady had known specific information about him that she could not possibly know. He was awestruck, and very pleased, because she'd said he would find his voice, become a published writer, and travel to exotic locales. She warned him about a brown haired, green eyed stranger who was to be avoided at all costs. Eddie thought about the people he knew but none really fit the description except maybe Mark in Honolulu. Were his eyes green? Blue/green? He wasn't really a stranger either. He drove back feeling like the car was floating above the road. He parked and went up to his room. There was a note that had been slipped under the door.

 "Party 2night–our place."

 –Rich

 Instead of going though Eddie made some notes in his notebook about the day, read a little, grew weary, and fell asleep. In the morning he was the first at the buffet piling on the pancakes and bacon. Today he planned on delivering Dr. Kublar's letter to a Mrs. Carlyle at an address in the Hollywood Hills. He called from the lobby, a man answered: "Mrs. Carlyle's residence." Eddie stated his reason for calling. He was asked to wait. The man came back on to ask he could arrive at 2 PM. He agreed, hung up, looked outside at the empty pool hoping Urs and Melanie would show up. Today was also the first day in the recording studio for Wolf Snake at 3:30 PM. He looked at a map and thought he could easily do both. He spent the rest of the morning reading, by the pool....

12

Mrs. Carlyle's house in the Hollywood Hills was impressive and surrounded by greenery including a grand Italian Cypress on either side of the entrance. Eddie parked his rental in the wide driveway. Outside of the car he looked the place over. As pretty as it was there was something haunted about it he thought, some aura, or was he still enchanted after the session with the fortune teller? Eddie pressed the buzzer at the front door, and heard a chime echo inside. The door swung open to a older black man in a butler uniform. The funny part Eddie thought was that the man needed a shave. His white whiskers obvious, his tie a bit askew, and if Eddie was right, he'd had a few nips already.

"Good afternoon. May I help you seer, I mean sar, I mean sir sorry sir."

"I'm here to see Mrs. Carlyle at 2 PM. Edward Knox for Dr. Kublar," Eddie said and thinking: oh brother what is this? The butler nevertheless gestured him in, through a dark foyer, into a room out of a gothic mystery, a room for Count Dracula. He watched Eddie's reaction. The butler seeming to have regained his wherewithal and explained:

"All props and furnishings are from Mrs. Carlyle's last great horror films: The Black Mansion, and The Black Mansion II."

"Most impressive."

There was a low ember fire in an elaborate fireplace since no natural light entered the room. The ceilings were so high, the fire made sense. With a sudden chill Eddie approached its warmth followed by the butler who crouched, and jabbed at it with a poker like he was killing a snake. He finally stopped, and added some new logs.

"Please relax Mr. Knox. I will bring you some refreshments shortly. Mrs. Carlyle received an important telephone call just moments ago, and so she will unfortunately be delayed. She does hope you will understand."

"Of course. I'll enjoy this room," Eddie said touching a Ouija board there on a table, but flinching in afterthought, not wanting to offend any lingering spirits. The butler shuffled off down a semi-dark hallway. Eddie took a look around the room. He examined a life size sculpture of a raven. He studied a painting that threatened to pull him in to its jungle of jeweled spider webs and mists. At the bookshelf he marveled over the selection. A selection that could rival Kublar's: but books on the film industry, biographies, travel photo books, art books, olden tomes on the occult, ancient civilizations, gilt-edged supernatural fiction and mysteries galore. Eddie was about to pull out a slim slightly cracked, leather-bound volume with "Arthur Machen" carved into the spine when the butler, whom Eddie hadn't heard approaching, startled him with a throat clearing and an announcement:

"Mrs. Carlyle will be down presently. Please Mr. Knox may I make you a cocktail."

The butler now had a cart on wheels in front of him and was wearing white gloves.

"Thank you, but it's early for me. I'll have some mineral water please."

"As you wish." The butler shot some soda water from an old time siphon into a tall glass. "Ice?"

"No, thank you." Eddie accepted the drink, and took a seat on a shiny black bench.

"Will there be anything else s-sir?" the butler asked. Eddie said no that he was content.

Eddie drank the water greedily having become dry. Putting the glass down seemed to stir dust in the air, since he could see it on everything. He imagined a microscopic, constant swirl of it in the haunted house, a heaven for dust mites. He felt a little drowsy, and was fighting it when a woman's voice roused him.

"There you are dear boy. I'm so sorry to have kept you waiting. Please forgive me. I hope Russell has taken care of you sufficiently?"

Eddie got to his feet, and introduced himself to a woman he was sure was in her eighties, or even nineties. She was an obvious recipient of massive plastic surgery. Her skin so tight that from a distance one would assume her to be a woman maybe half that age. He couldn't get over the feeling that Mrs. Carlyle might not be real at all, but no, she was just wrapped so tightly in her own skin that she appeared startling at first. She could not smile nor make any facial expressions. He would find she expressed herself best with her eyes, and some gestures.

"Hello Edward. May I call you Edward? Please take that chair and Russell, bring me a chair immediately!"

Eddie was taken aback at the stern command in her voice, and by Russell's quick subservient manner as he pushed an identical chair that Eddie was standing by so she could simply fall back into it. Eddie took out Dr. Kublar's letter, presented it to her, then took his seat. She smiled, or rather smiled with her eyes, and called out:

"Russell! Now!"

Russell appeared like an apparition it seemed to Eddie. He bowed, asked:

"Mistress?"

"A letter opener, my glasses and a lamp. Now!"

Russell, seemed again to Eddie's eyes, to disappear when he looked away for a second. Eddie felt maybe he should pinch himself to return to reality. The room was dark, in shadows, dim amber lights pulsed from the corners.

"Russell has been with me for over twenty years. Can you imagine? Don't fret about how I deal with him. It's not my idea, rather his. A born masochist I'm afraid, and if I try and deal with him civilly he pouts and won't perform his chores. A ridiculous situation that I go along with. I must admit over the years it has come to amuse me. I love Russell dearly as I know he does me, but, well, there you have it. He does come to me on occasion to simply talk about the old days, but before long wants me pushing him around again."

"Curious, and fascinating, like everything in this place," Eddie remarked, then wondered if he'd said too much but Mrs. Carlyle laughed.

"You're probably wondering how I met Dr. Kublar whom I assume you're studying under?"

"Yes, in a sense. And yes, I'd love to hear if you don't mind telling me."

"This was forty some years ago. I was a dancer then. I hadn't done any real acting. I was only included in some crowd shots. But, one producer picked me out from a crowd and wanted to see me privately. I found that he wanted to see me because he wanted to fuck me."

Eddie laughed at her frankness, and was beginning to warm up to this interesting old friend of the doctor's. He glanced at the fireplace and in that split second Russell reappeared adjusting a lamp for Mrs. Carlyle. She said:

"It certainly took you long enough! Leave us alone now!"

"Y-yes mistress," Russell uttered, bowing, backing away and shuffling down the hallway. Mrs. Carlyle called out: "Quietly!" And sure enough the shuffling sound stopped.

"So, I escaped the arms of this horny producer by the skin of my teeth, but this only egged him on. He began sending me flowers, and limos to take me home and pick me up in the morning for work. Silly girl that I was I became frightened by all of this and felt I was being pressured to screw the old coot. The supernatural film that I had been given a decent speaking role began production. The director called in some experts on the occult as consultants. He interviewed a number of them, and Dr. Kublar, a young man then, was chosen. He cut quite a figure in those days. People said he was a combination Tesla, Houdini, Crowley and Dali. Some of the other actors were attracted to him, yet others found his magnetism disturbing. He was full of energy, sported a waxed Van Dyke, and wore tailored black suits with red satin shirts. A large ruby beamed from his middle finger. They called him Lucifer behind his back. I think he enjoyed that.

"One day as I was sulking and worrying about how I was going to handle myself in the situation with the producer, I felt a presence, and looked up to find Dr. Kublar staring at me intensely. He sat next to me, took my hand and said: 'I will help you with your troubles. Confide in me and you will come out the winner in this nonsense that is troubling you.' I believed and trusted him right away, and after the day's work he came to my bungalow. I told him the story and he laid out exactly what I was to do. Rather than explain each step of what he taught me, the main thrust was he made me see that as a woman I had the potential to be a powerful witch, and that I could turn the situation, manipulate it if you like, into a success. I had to overcome my own insecurities, and break down the rigid mindset imprinted on me by parents, teachers and society, and then use the new weapons at my disposal wisely.

"Within a week I was given the leading role. The girl who'd had it was a real bitch, and had been mean to me, so I was very pleased. I had the producer eating out of my hand and following me around like a zombie. This led to bigger roles, and bigger producers until I arrived at a point I could ditch them all. Do you find it satanic?"

"Well, no. Rational really."

"Exactly, and that's what the doctor would say: you are now following your rational self. The irrational is important as well especially to an artist. Eddie, there are good people, and there are bad people basically, generally. We know this of course, but some can trick you, so you must develop an inner detector. Your guardian's voice is that detector, among other things. It's always with you. You need to connect. I can help you with that here." Then Russell was back whispering something in her ear. She tapped him on the nose, and rolled up her sleeve.

"Time for my morphine," she said. Russell rolled his tray back over and prepared to give her an injection.

Expect for a soft "...ahh," when the tie was released and the plunger was pushed there was no noticeable change in her. But Eddie thought, how could there be? Except for the eyes. It was all about her eyes, and they were beautiful, large and gray blue. The pupils, dilated from the morphine, showed that she was rejoicing, replenishing her cells, enjoying being brought back to life. She clapped her hands twice.

"More refreshments!"

For some reason Eddie brought up his experience with the fortune teller. Hearing himself speak of it had a curious effect on him, as though he was stepping deep into another dimension or alternate world. Russell refilled the glasses.

"Be gone now! Out of sight, but pay attention to my beckoned call! You hear me?"

"Y-yes mistress," Russell uttered backing away.

Mrs. Carlyle was like a bizarre queen from some impossible distant planet. She was studying Eddie with those wondrous eyes. He told her more about the reading, and when he'd finished Mrs. Carlyle said:

"But of course dear lad. You were drawn to Lady Hazeli. I

know her quite well. She does my readings here. In fact she sits in the chair you're now sitting in."

Eddie found that a little unsettling at first, but skipped that for the feeling of being attuned to this world that he was becoming more familiar with.

Mrs. Carlyle sipped her drink with a straw, and winked.

"You are in the best of hands for your education, and entrance to the world of the guardian recipients. You will learn how to summon your guardian voice at any time. Are you ready to learn your code?"

"Yes, sure, of course," Eddie said setting the glass down, folding his hands in front of him, wondering what was next.

"Russell! The helmet! Now!"

Russell wheeled in a different tray, more of a table. On it sat a macabre looking helmet with blinking blue and white lights intertwined on wires, and covered with rows of plug-ins. It was like a deep sea diving helmet, redesigned for inner space travel? Russell made some adjustments on a control board. A screen showing ever changing graphs emerged. The sounds of radio static were emitted, and various bleeps like an old sci fi film. Russell lifted the helmet. Eddie remained still as he placed it over his head. He found it surprisingly comfortable, snug, with a briny ocean smell. In a WHOOSH moment he was standing on a bleak, misty shore looking out to a viking ship at sea...a conch shell sounded...behind him was a magnificent mountain ringed in pink mist...another wild conch call echoed...he walked toward a deep cave....

Inside the cave was a replica of the room he was in, but instead of Mrs. Carlyle...an incredible young woman, nearly naked, who looked to Eddie to have stepped from some fabulous legend...jet black hair...flashing dark eyes...twirling a strand of hair in her fingers...smiling....

"Edward," her voice at first echoed as through a vast tunnel.

"Edward...I will guide you u u u ...I am you in a sense. Ifanititifanbidit. To call me remember that: Ifanititifanbidit. Say it."

"Ifanititifanbidit."

"Say it again and again and again."

"Ifanititifanbidit, ifanititifanbidit, infan... "

She approached in slow motion...singing it along with him in a soft, sing song voice...she touched his hands that were at his side...

"Be alone...no disturbances...close thy eyes...chant thy chant within...it will give you strentgh...it will give you time travel... when you see the red light a door appears...there is a handle...I will come, mostly in voice...sometimes like this...I love you Eddie...I was made to love you...sensations were over taking him, and then something shifted...he was looking out a window... traveling trough space...in a kind of space train...two black leopards were with him in the car...they sat by him and purred...Eddie felt something funny in his head...the scene vanished...he was looking at the room again...

Russell was holding the helmet with a blank expression. "Mrs. Carlyle had to leave," he said.

"That was too far out man!" Eddie said brightly.

"The mistress has instructed me to bid you farewell, and the best of luck. She immensely enjoyed meeting you, and helping you along your way. She instructed me to tell you that you are a welcome guest anytime you happen to be in LA. She gives you this: a return letter for Dr. Kublar."

Eddie put the letter in his inner jacket pocket, glanced at his wristwatch. He saw that three hours had passed. He could have sworn he'd been there no more than a half hour. He told Russell he would find his own way out. Russell, lost in fidgeting with the machine nodded. Outside Eddie felt like he was back in the world of reality. It was something of a comedown, but he decided that two worlds were better than one. And now, like all the characters that populated the fables he had read as a child, he too was privy to a secret world. He figured the recording session was over, but as the sun set over Hollywood mixing wildly with the sky's pollution he followed the directions to the studio's address. It was in an out of the way industrial neighborhood with some bums sleeping against walls and other shady characters lurking about.

There was a massive, bald black guy at the entrance who blocked Eddie's way even when he told him he was part of the band's crew and entourage. The giant told him he would have to check it out first. He shut the industrial door behind him. A few minutes later he opened it and let Eddie in. Down a dimly lit hallway he came to a waiting room with gold records, framed photos of music artists lining the walls. At the front desk, in the reception area sat a blonde talking on a phone. At first Eddie thought it was Melanie. She pointed to another hallway and continued her phone conversation with somebody who was making her laugh. Eddie passed a room that held two pool tables, chairs, and vending machines but empty of people. Further back he came to two doors, one to the control room, the other to a studio where the band was sitting on stools wearing headphones.

Richmond let Eddie into the control booth that turned out to be fairly roomy. He spotted Connie asleep in a corner on a bean bag chair. At the control boards sat a greasy looking guy in a suit with long hair that looked like it needed a wash. Next to him was a heavy set guy with maybe a couple day's growth of facial hair nearly busting out of a Suzi Quatro T-shirt. They both glanced at Eddie without much interest. Eddie took a seat in the back next to Richmond who fired up a doobie. He took a few deep hits before handing it to him.

"Where you been man? We thought you got lost," he said in that repressed voice one has while holding in smoke. "You've been missing some wild times," he said normally after the exhale.

"Yeah, sorry, I met these girls and then this woman and..."

"Whoa Eddie you old horn dog. Why 'doncha bring 'em around?"

"It's complicated, but maybe later. I have the girl's number. How's the recording going?"

The heavy set dude turned and shushed them. A moment later the room filled with music. It was a drumless number with fast acoustic guitar strumming Eddie was not familiar with. Yet right away he heard the Glam rock influence he had turned Richmond onto. When the playback ended the big guy said into a mike:

"How did that sound? Do you wanna do another take?"

Richmond said: "No, it's perfect." He jumped up, went into the main room, and came back with the rest of the band.

"That's it," Richmond repeated. "Keep it and keep the other takes just in case. The fat guy and the greasy guy looked at each other with no particular expression, nodded. The greasy guy said: "So, what's next Rich?"

"We want to do one more today, something of an experiment. We have the music but not the words. We want to wing it, see how it comes out." The greasy guy made a face. The rest of the band made comments about how it could be great. They all agreed to listen to the songs they'd recorded, and then decide if they wanted to try one more. Everyone sat back, closed their eyes, and the first track: "Polk Street Shuffle," came on with its sped up Chuck Berry riff, Matt's howling vocals, and a rhythm section that reminded Eddie of a runaway train. Everyone smiled as it screeched to an end. Eddie was impressed as the songs unfolded. He felt he was indeed in the presence of rock 'n roll greatness.

There was another Glam influenced number, but Wolf Snake's edgy, rawness on the other tunes reminded Eddie more of of The Stooges or The MC5, or at times as if the Doors and the Sonics had collaborated. Brilliant, Eddie thought. The band seemed pleased too. Eddie was to learn that there had been a crowd of hangers on, drug dealers, and party people earlier, but they'd kicked everybody out since no work was getting done.

Newly inspired, they all agreed they wanted to give the unwritten number a go. Eddie suggested keeping it an instrumental, but only Diamond Jack liked that idea. They went back into the recording room after the other band members did some bumps of coke, tokes from a joint, and swigs of bourbon. Richmond and Eddie took a pass on the C and the Wild Turkey, and so did the producer and engineer who seemed perfectly content with their cigarettes, soft drinks and junk food. They went back in the studio to record the track. Matt would add the vocals once he came up with lyrics. He stayed behind with Eddie.

"Usually I just sings anything until the lyrics come to me, but with this tune nothing's happening." He looked at Eddie brightly. "Hey, *you're* a writer. Why not take a crack at it?"

"I never wrote any lyrics, but sure, I'll try something."

Matt and Eddie put on head phones, and listened to the band run through it. The big guy signaled for another take. Eddie was handed a tablet, a pen by the now somewhat annoyed engineer. He had become agitated for some unknown reason. Eddie found out later he was also the minder for the label. Eddie nestled himself into a corner, and closed his eyes as the track was played, then replayed, and played again. He cleared his head and wrote down what his subconscious spoke:

You got a red light baby. You got a red light on me.
You got a red light baby. You got a red light on me.
I wanna change your direction and make your driving time speed.
yeah speed
I was a lonely driver I was cruising on my own
I was a lonely driver I was wasted, I was stoned
But then I ran that red light, and I'm looking for your love love driver yeah!

I got a green light honey I got a green light on you
I got a green light honey, and I'm driving straight on through
I will change your direction I will change it through and through
love driver yeah!
(repeat)

Eddie handed the tablet to Matt who laughed and said:
"Fuck, Eddie this is good!"

Eddie sang it along with another playback, showed Matt where he could do his famous mike breathing that Eddie had noticed wasn't on the other cuts. He found out later that the band had voted it down, but Eddie felt it was a mistake to not use it at all. Matt said:

"Eddie my man, you are a genius, and you have a nice voice as well. Why not do some double vocals on it? We can trash them if they don't work out."

Eddie agreed and went into the studio with Matt, who got no resistance since everybody was ready to see it happen. Eddie was directed into a booth, and shown by Matt how to sing into the mike. After a couple of partial run throughs, and one last minute change, "Love Driver" was finished to great applause from the rest of the band and even the label guy. The fat Suzi Quatro loving producer smiled and said it was damn good and ballsy. Richmond told Eddie that if they used it, he would get credit for the lyrics and performance. Eddie found that exciting and wondered if maybe music was another creative pursuit he should explore. Everyone was telling him he was a natural.

That night he slept in an extra hour. The phone was ringing when he came out of the shower: Richmond telling him that Wolf Snake was going to play a private party along with two local bands and that he should inform his lady friends.

13

Eddie decided to take a swim since it looked like he would have the pool to himself. He swam the length of the pool, back and forth. When he climbed out and began to towel off he noticed that someone was sitting behind a newspaper, in a chair at the other end, and he smelled cigar. As Eddie walked by the man he dropped his paper and said good morning. He was heavy set, wearing a bathrobe, and bedroom slippers. He reminded Eddie of Sidney Greenstreet from the classic noir films.

"Could I have a word with you Mr. Knox?" he said, startling Eddie who was on his way to catch the elevator.

"Sorry, do I know you?" Eddie asked forgetting the elevator.

"Well, no. I represent a collector of fine antiquities who is in the process of finalizing a purchase of an ancient Chinese head sculpture. One that you are listed as the owner."

"Mister?"

"Mr. Buckhorn," he said putting his cigar into an ashtray. He extended a chubby hand and gave Eddie a quick yet firm shake.

"How did'ya know I was here? Staying here? Weren't you given my San Francisco address?" Eddie asked with a tweak of suspicion in his tone.

"I did try and talk with you there, at Dr. Kublar's residence in Chinatown where you have your apartment. I was told you had come here with the rock band. The rest was easy and since I had other business here I thought I'd kill two birds, you know."

"Mr. Buckhorn, I need to shower, get dressed, and then I can meet you in the lobby. We could have coffee in the café if you'd like."

"A wonderful idea," Buckhorn said. "I need to change myself. I'll see you in thirty minutes then."

Eddie hurried over to the elevator that had just opened expelling a family of noisy Italians. He was a bit unnerved by Mr. Buckhorn showing up like this. It didn't seem business like. He called Dr. Kublar but got no answer. He dressed, and looked at himself in the mirror wondering how he'd come to this place in his life and what the future had in store. He found Mr. Buckhorn sitting in a comfortable chair in the café that was part of the lobby. He was dressed in a Panama suit, white shirt, red bow tie; a straw hat sat on his lap. He was listening to a young Hispanic boy who was gesturing wildly as he talked. Mr. Buckhorn was smiling. When Eddie approached the boy fled, Mr. Buckhorn laughed. Eddie took a chair.

"A crazy little bugger. Telling wild tales of spies and counterfeiters, and that his own step-dad is involved. A born writer I believe that kid is, like you."

"Now where did you hear that?"

"Mr. Knox, my employer, expects a background check so thorough it would make Interpol envious. I know more about you than you know, but please don't worry about that skipping out on probation. Your case has since been dropped, buried even, and my investigation shows that you were like a lot of restless youths, a casualty of a corrupt justice system. As to your writing, a piece you wrote for your college English class was published in an underground newspaper in Harrisburg. Quite good too I thought. Mr. Neil Stanton wanted me to give you a copy."

Mr. Buckhorn went through his briefcase, came up with the newspaper, handed it over. On the front of: The Magic Frog was a psychedelic drawing that reminded him of Medusa. Eddie skimmed the contents and found The Escape Artist by Edward Knox, and he felt a slight thrill. He thanked Mr. Buckhorn who was getting the attention of a passing waitress. He ordered a small pot of coffee, and two Danish.

"Now back to your most fortunate find at ye olde flea market," Buckhorn said with an involuntary corrupt smile. "Mr. Garret and Dr. Kublar have conveyed the story, but I must hear it from your lips. All the documents that needed signed have been signed, everything else is in order."

"Well, I've always had a thing for flea markets," Eddie said. "I'd found a new apartment in the city and thought maybe I could find some items for it. I had a painting in mind, but at one vendor's stand I was drawn to that head which was set back, and mostly obscured by some piles of papers. His regular display as I recall was mostly appliances: old phones, blenders, toasters and such. When he saw I was interested he cleaned it off, and priced it at ten dollars which I gladly paid. It was a heavy thing. I was glad to get it back to my apartment. I found it rather gruesome, but fascinating. I definitely felt an ancient vibe from it. And then Dr. Kublar noticed it, and you know the rest."

"And which flea market was this?" Eddie named the place. Mr. Buckhorn looked at a small notebook and said:

"Very good. I'm curious if you think the original owner should get any money?"

"Yes, I do, and I returned to that flea market to locate him, to get his name, but I couldn't find him. He wasn't at the spot he'd been. The other regulars in that area didn't know anything about him. They said he'd only been there once or maybe twice. I checked with the registry. They had no record of him and said that he must've been a rogue." Eddie actually had done all of that at the doctor's insistence.

The coffee, milk, sugar, and pastries arrived as well as slices of cantaloupe. The fruit looked stiff to Eddie, as though it had been refrigerated too long. Dr. Buckhorn insisted on paying, and tipped the waitress generously.

"Very good, Mr. Knox, and so nice to make your acquaintance. My business is done here now, and I thank you again. How do you like Los Angeles?"

"I'm enjoying it. A vast city on wheels that seems to be pushing itself further into a doomed future." Mr. Buckhorn laughed.

When Eddie arrived at the band's hotel he caught them heading to two parked limousines. The greasy label guy from the studio was standing by one wearing the same suit. Eddie climbed into the second limo with Matt, Richmond, and a knockout blonde who was introduced as Sherry. She winked at Eddie, and crossed her shapely legs. She was wearing a micro-mini, white platforms, and black/white striped stockings. Her hair was platinum in a longish shag. She wore a pink satin jacket, a big Wolf Snake button. Her makeup looked applied by a stylist with a bit of silver glitter on her prominent cheekbones. It became obvious that she was Matt's groupie, especially when she began rubbing his crotch.

"Later Sherry baby, later."

"You're not embarrassed in front of your mates are you? What kind of a rock star are you?" she teased. "I want to suck you off in the limo bay bee." She started to unzip him; Matt sat back, said, "Go ahead. Knock yourself out." Richmond who sat across from Eddie said:

"Don't mind them. We're stopping at Fredrick's of Hollywood, and then we're to do a radio interview. You're coming to the show tonight?'

"Natch."

Matt started grunting; Sherry was making m-m-m-m- sounds and then Matt went Ahhhhhhhh. Sherry pulled off with a splat of cum on her pretty mug. She laughed, wiped it off. Matt cleaned himself up too with some Kleenex, tossed it out the window. "How about you two?" Sherry asked licking her lower lip. Matt said: "Hold on there girly. Do you want me to ever kiss you?" She laughed, sat on his lap, kissed him. The driver pulled over, and parked.

"Here's the place kids. Let's go."

Inside was a bunch of tacky clothes crowding racks, some areas displaying fantastic gear like pointed bras, stripper clothes, fancy stockings, in short, seduction gear. Matt bought Sherry some lacey lingerie. Nathan, their photographer who looked like the dude on Bambu rolling papers took some pictures of the band mugging next to cardboard replicas of scantily clad Bettie Page and Marilyn Monroe. Then everyone piled back into the limos that headed next for the radio station.

Eddie, Sherry and Nathan sat in the waiting room at the station, and listened to the interview, which was pretty funny. The disc jockey played a raw mix of "Love Driver," that startled Eddie for a second, but in a good way. Hearing his lyrics, and his voice seemed unreal. Afterward they ended up at Schwabs Pharmacy for coffee and ice cream sodas. On the ride back joints were lit, and Matt and Sherry did toots of coke. The limos parked in front, at the hotel. Everyone was in a good mood, talking about the show later that evening. But the mood died as a gang of police came out of the entrance, followed by a gurney pushed with a corpse covered in a sheet.

They were approached by someone Eddie took for a detective, and he was right. The detective said loudly: "I need to talk to everyone who is staying in rooms 306, 307 and 412, the band Wolf Shakes and anyone who visited those rooms." Richmond corrected him on the band's name, and asked what the hell had happened.

"And who are you?"

"Richmond Saunders, drummer and acting manager for the

band."

"Well, I certainly want to talk with you, and everybody else in your group, friends, visitors, hangers on, the works."

"What happened?"

"There's been a death by overdose, a Miss Connie Wells, who is one of the registered guests for room 307. She still had the spike in her arm. The maid found her on the floor. Did you know she was a dope addict?"

"She was clean. She was recovering. This trip was to help her get away from her connections, and junky friends in San Francisco. She—" Richmond turned to look as the corpse was being loaded into the van, sighed, didn't say any more. The detective looked at Eddie who was standing with them and said: "And who are you?"

"Edward Knox, friend of the band."

"Are you staying in one of those room too?"

"No, I'm not staying here. I haven't even been to their rooms."

"Did you know the deceased?"

"I met her once, if you consider that knowing her. I don't."

Diamond Jack and the others had gathered around. Sherry was standing to the side with Nathan the photographer. Eddie noticed that her makeup was smeared from crying. She had taken off her shoes and was holding them by the straps. Eddie would find out later that she'd never met Connie. Another cop in a plaid suit joined the other detective. They huddled with a uniformed cop, then the first one turned around and announced:

"Okay folks we want to ask you all to come inside. The hotel has given us a room to take statements." Eddie remembered Connie at the recording studio. She was probably smacked out then. Richmond had been too preoccupied with the recording to pay her much mind, probably figuring her sleeping was good for getting through the late withdrawal. Once in a room that usually served as a conference room, tables were set up, people took seats. One by one they were called in to join a detective in another smaller adjacent room. Eventually Eddie was called in by the newer cop, a short guy with a mop of brown curly hair. He wore glasses, with thick black frames. He smelled of English Leather, his shirt sleeves were too long; he had an acne problem and gave off a brusk, impatient vibe. His walk was reminiscent of Groucho Marx.

"Have a seat, Knox," he said, sitting above on a table top.

"Are you the dope dealer?"

"Excuse me? Are you trying to be funny?"

"Do I look like I'm being funny? This could easily turn into murder one for the scum who gave that young lady a hot shot."

"Of course I'm not a dope dealer. I'm a music fan and friend of Richmond's, er Mr. Saunders, the band's spokesman."

"Do you have any kind of a record?" Eddie hoped what Mr. Buckhorn said was true, that his record had been buried, and decided to throw the detective a curve ball.

"I don't have a record. I told you I'm a fan not a musician. They are here making a record."

Eddie could see the confusion traveling around in his face.

"Not that kind of a record, a criminal record!"

"Of course not."

"We'll check that. And where were you joy birds in your fancy limos today?"

Eddie remained calm. He told the cop where they had been, leaving out Sherry giving Jack a blow job and snorting coke. He also had to state where he was staying.

"Can I see your arms?" the cop asked with an suspicious look. Eddie laughed, and said sure. The cop looked disappointed at finding not one track mark, although he kept looking as if one was somehow hiding from him. "What a pervert," Eddie was thinking as he rolled his sleeve back down, and asked if he was done. Just about then the first detective came in and said:

"Oh, don't bother with him. We've found the dealer." He took his partner aside but Eddie could still hear him.

"Not related to the band at all. Local asshole, works the strip and when bands come to town. We picked him up shooting pool at Barney's Beanery."

14

Eddie decided to try the Japanese restaurant a few doors down. He had never had Japanese food. Immediately he liked what he saw: the decor, music, kimonoed waitresses with geisha makeup and chopsticks in their hair. From this experience Eddie would develop an interest in Japanese culture, read some of the writers, and study yakuza and samurai films. He tried some sushi, and sipped sake before diving into his salmon teriyaki and tempura. Afterward, back at his room he called Melanie, but no one answered.

Eddie parked the rental in a lot, and walked a couple blocks to the warehouse where the gig was. In front of the place, groups of hipsters huddled here and there, smoking, all into the Glam look. At the entrance the same bouncer from the recording studio stood with a guy who looked like an albino biker, arms folded, a blank expression. The first bouncer who had a friendly look said, "He's cool. He's with the headliners." Eddie nodded, and continued in, deciding not to stop for any meaningless chit chat. The room was packed and he had trouble maneuvering himself through it to get back stage. He finally made it to the back stage door. A bouncer he didn't know was blocking the way, a tall white guy who reminded him of a hippie lumberjack or a mountain man.

"Whoa right there palsy. Nobody gets back heah."

Eddie flashed him the special stamp he received at the second entrance where they checked for your name on a list. The bouncer looked around as if to be sure no one was looking, said: "Okay now!" practically pushing him through. He walked down a badly lit industrial stairway to the lower level that was also crowded with groups standing around talking. In the last of three rooms on the right side of the corridor he found Richmond drumming on a cardboard box, Diamond Jack fingering his unplugged guitar, and some girl who looked like a zombie sitting on the floor .

"Eddie, come in and shut the fucking door."

"Hey hi! How are you?"

"OK...you know, the show must go on," Richmond said. "We can work out our shit through the music. It's one time we don't have to think, just be, you know, man?"

"Sure, you have the right idea. The place is packed and the last band just finished up."

Diamond Jack shared the information that two other locals in the LA music scene had OD'd on the same batch of dope. One was the lead singer of the well loved group Huntress who were originally to headline. The other was her boyfriend and lead guitarist. "That's why the crowd is so big. It's something of a wake," Diamond Jack said. "We iz ready to deliver thee goods. We 'ad a meeting earlier: dress all in black an balls out," Jack concluded, looking particularly cadaverous himself.

"Outstanding. I can't wait to hear you."

The label guy opened the door.

"Let's go boys. We need to get ready."

Eddie said good luck, did a new handshake that Diamond Jack showed him where you let your open hand slide against the other guy's without gripping, then lightly bump fists. Richmond gave Eddie a biker's hug. Diamond Jack shrugged, and did the same. The zombie girl stood and walked out.

When Wolf Snake took the dimly lit stage Eddie swore he could feel the energy and mood escalating, and teetering on the brink of massive release through the controlled chaos that this band could deliver. The crowd needed Wolf Snake and Wolf Snake needed the crowd. Matt took the mike off the stand, and stepped to the edge of the stage. He crouched down, motionless. He'd changed from his usual vest and untucked white shirt and tight, black jeans to an all leather outfit with a motorcycle jacket. The turned up collar made him look like a classic fifties delinquent.

"We dedicate this set to our dearly departed friend Connie Wells, to the great Cindy Hampton, and to the equally great Ned Barrett. The crowd roared, Matt bowed his head and when the crowd quieted he began to prowl around the stage to whoops and screeches. He stopped and called out: "We call this SF Strut" but tonight it's "LA Strut!" The crowd went wild and were overtaken by something akin to the force of a jet engine from this band, all dressed in black. Once the number screeched to a halt, the crowd went crazier. Eddie felt a body rush, and thought their live sound was the best he'd ever heard. They were like giants and making the sound of giants. The band launched into another number: "Buzz Buzz Buzz". The brutal metallic assault continued with a beat that shook the walls for the next thirty minutes. Wolf Snake's performance was a rock 'n roll show so incredible and brutal that Eddie felt like he was being born again. It was as though some ancient pagan ritual had traveled through space and time and was being reenacted. For that night Wolf Snake was the greatest rock 'n roll band in the world. There was no encore since they had demolished most of their equipment: Diamond Jack had smashed his Les Paul copy into pieces with a hammer while Richmond kicked over and trashed his drum kit, and then proceeded to piss on the wreckage. Pitt's forehead had been slashed by one of Jack's guitar strings when they'd been flailing about. He looked demonic with the blood dripping down his face, and stood staring upward like a man possessed. A crowd gathered around him, and put their hands on him, moaning in ecstasy.

Eddie started to leave, but felt a hand on his arm. He turned to find Melanie and Urs looking spectacularly Glam but grim. They'd been crying and they hugged Eddie desperately. Later he found out that Cindy and Ned had been good friends of theirs. And so, even with the catharsis of the show, and the completion of the record over the next couple of days, the mood was somber on the flight home. At SFO Eddie went off on his own, and had a Bloody Mary at the airport bar before going outside and getting a cab back home.

* * *

As Eddie was letting himself into his small Chinatown apartment he heard someone behind him. He turned expecting to see Mu, but instead found a man dressed as a woman, wearing frumpy clothes, a wig, and glasses. He was holding a small white pocketbook. The man's mouth was partially open.

"I'm sorry to have startled you. Actually you gave me a start although I did expect you this week." Eddie's confused expression caused the man to say:

"Sorry, I'm Beth Robbins, well my real name is Robert but, well, you see," he smiled sheepishly. "I like to play. I just get a thrill dressing like this, and you can see I'm not fooling anybody. I don't want to. That's part of the thrill. And San Francisco is heaven for me. I'm enjoying my stay here immensely. I'm from Austin by the way. I do prefer you to refer to me as Beth. Is that okay? I'm the translator?"

When Eddie was finally given a chance to speak he offered a hand and said:

"Well, pleased to meet you Beth. I'm Eddie Knox and I rent—"

"Oh, I know all about you Eddie. The doctor spoke wondrously about you. A writer yes?"

"Trying to be. I feel it in my bones." That made Beth laugh heartily, although Eddie was perplexed as to why. Beth regained his composure:

"The doctor and Mu went to New York. They'll be there another week or so."

The next morning Eddie dressed, but avoided the Glam gear in his wardrobe. He'd seen so much of it in LA he felt more in tune with Wolf Snake's idea to wear all black. Eddie had listened to Richmond on the plane explaining the decision to wear all black at the gig for a funeral mood. Eddie had urged him to get the band to stick with it. It suited them, and would make them stand apart. Eddie pointed out that all the other bands now looked the same, imitating the British in one way or another, and not always successfully, although The New York Dolls did a striking version all their own, sort of like if the Stones were in their prime, and exploited the mood of when they had done that drag photo. Eddie explained that Wolf Snake would automatically stick out for being different. The sound they had presented at the show was also pure brilliance.

"You owned that crowd. You were the Pied Pipers of rock 'n roll. You should always strive to achieve that again. Being true to yourselves like you were that night is the road to being a success. I don't mean record sales or rock stardom, those are only the trappings. What you did that night is what success is all about."

Richmond had looked at him as though he'd just discovered something magical about him. He looked at Eddie the way Eddie sometimes looked at Dr. Kublar.

"Fuckin' Eddie. You're dynamite man. You surprise me more and more. Are you a practitioner of the black arts maybe?"

"Yes," Eddie said and they both had a laugh.

So today, Eddie, put on a black Mod suit, a gray and black striped shirt, and pulled on his now scuffy beatle boots. He looked at himself in the mirror. He realized he was aging by increments that could not be seen by the human eye. He thought: the mirror must be explored! Perhaps if one could stare into the mirror long enough one could learn some truth? And so he moved the small table into the bath so he could stare into the mirror until he felt something. Eddie laughed at himself then because he wasn't even high. He was ready to abandon the project all together when he remembered Dr. Kublar's words: "When you discover something that your inner self discovers, and then laughs at, pay close attention. There's usually something to be learned and gained there."

How much time had passed with Eddie staring at himself in the mirror he didn't know. Time seemed to have lost its grip on him, and space threatened to do the same. He felt he was passing through different levels of consciousness. His face began to change. He became older, and older and older, and it became hard to look. Like Dorian Gray, he thought, then he wasn't there at all. He kept staring into the blackness until a white sperm wiggled into view, penetrated a female egg that had also appeared, and then an embryo formed. It floated there before him, morphing into a jellyfish then an infant, a child, a strange creature, a young boy, a wolf, a teenager, and now, and now—he was glowing; he saw a minute change on his face, an almost imperceptible indentation on his cheek that would be missed by the naked eye. The glow faded and Eddie was looking at himself again normally. He wiped some sweat off his neck. He knew where that mark was. He could now see it if he looked carefully. It was then that Eddie decided to become a long term hedonist rather than a short term one, something else the good doctor had advised him on.

Eddie wandered around Chinatown, enjoying the familiar smells and sights. He knew the streets, back alleys and the place in general fairly well now, but he longed for another visit underground. He headed to a noodle restaurant he liked for a light lunch. Before he arrived he noticed a photo in the street by the curb, between two parked cars. He stopped to pick it up. He'd started a collection of found photographs. He wasn't sure why he collected them, but he figured they would help him in his writing somehow, or at least he wanted to experiment with them in some way. He wiped the dirt off the one he'd picked up. It was a Chinese woman looking straight into the camera with a somewhat maudlin expression. She was attractive enough, reminding him somehow of a femme fatale in a detective story. He felt that he knew her, or maybe he was going to meet her? Eddie was in a state of mind open to whatever the alternate universes had to offer him. He took a table at the noodle restaurant, and amidst the slurping noodle sounds, and the walls lined with tanks full of doomed, swimming fish, he continued to study the photograph.

Back at his apartment he sat down at the typewriter with his found photographs spread out on the bed like a hand of cards, as if they were a new kind of tarot. He took a few hits from a joint, and began to type while looking at the snapshots. When he was done he took the pages and sat on his bed to read them over. It was a story about the people in the photos as he'd imagined them in his mind. He had recently bought a framed cork board, and hung it on a wall. On it was an advert for a new club opening in North Beach called the Cabaret that proclaimed: "Where The Glam And Glitter Crowd Meet" above a photo of Brian Eno in full makeup and a feather boa. And there was a flyer for the Wolf Snake gig in LA with a crude drawing of a skull with a snake climbing out of an eye socket. He moved them to the side, pinned up the found photos he'd selected, and underneath them, his pages. He sat back on the bed, stared at them, and took a couple more hits from the joint. He made some brief notes in a steno book before starting to doze when a soft knock made him open his eyes.

"Who is it?"

"It's only me, Beth."

Eddie opened the door to find Beth in a new outfit, as bad and mad as the other, yet with different makeup. Eddie wondered if

Beth knew anything about Glam Rock.

"Eddie, I apologize, but I smelled something nice coming from your room and—it made me a little curious. I haven't smoked mary jane since college when I flirted briefly with the jazz and poetry scene, or what they called the Beats. Alas I never explored it enough, and quickly after graduation I went to work in the damn straight world. But, that led me to research, and I found I had a super mind, like a bee hive for information, especially for the arcane and esoteric. I also found I had a knack for translating ancient texts. I did a bit in Israel and Egypt for the government's archeology foundation, which was very exciting."

"Would you like to get high, Beth?"

"Could I smoke some with you?"

"Of course. Come in and have a seat."

Beth came in, sat and stared at Eddie's poster board and went hmmm.

"A writing experiment," Eddie said, re-lighting the joint, handing it to Beth. The lights were already dimmed. Eddie turned down the volume of Bowie's "Hunky Dory" album and told Beth to smoke it all since he was already high. He watched Beth's expression gradually change to a blissful one, and when he commented on the music Eddie handed him the album jacket, as well as "The Man Who Sold The World".

"Oh gosh," said Beth who stared and stared at the covers, and then back at Eddie; he finally asked, "What is this Eddie?"

He explained the Glam Rock movement. Beth looked to be fascinated. Eddie showed him the flyer for the Cabaret, said he was going later, and invited him to come along.

"Oh, I don't know. Thank you, but it might be too much, but hey, let me write down the address in case I change my mind. I do have some serious work to do tonight with the Tablet. It's proving to be a super challenge, but maybe now that I'm stoned. Hey, I'm stoned Eddie! This is nice. Wow!"

Eddie wrote down the address. He gave him a matchbox of weed and a little pipe he almost never used. Beth was thrilled with it all and kept thanking Eddie until he told him to stop.

"Let me take you out to lunch one day Eddie. Anywhere you'd like to go."

Eddie saw him to the door, and went back to his story typing out a few more pages. He thought about Beth as Robert in college listening to Bebop, visiting a coffee shop to hear beat poetry and rub shoulders with the hipsters. Eddie dug through his records, found an early Chet Baker album and put it on. He reclined, closed his eyes and repeated the chant that the guardian had taught him....

"Ifanititifanbidit. Ifan–"

red light...BOOM BOOM BOOM...red light...traffic light turning green...walking across the wet street in downtown? Where was he? He looked around: North Beach...still San Francisco... stopped at a newsstand: 1953...into a bar...beat, smoky bar filled with young men sporting goatees, svelte girls with short black hair, black turtlenecks...saw himself in a cloudy mirror...dressed in a wide striped jersey...James Dean style red jacket...bongos, a crazy trumpet began some cool school jazz...good looking beatnik girl reciting a poem on a small stage...acting it out, all animated... stressing words...the hipsters enthralled...saying yeah man...how long could he stay?...ride it Dr. Kublar had said...ride...he was sitting at a table looking at a candle in a Chianti bottle, the wax having dripped down its own art...a glass of red wine...accepted a rolled cigarette from a thin black guy wearing shades...a soft gray whispering suit...inhaled deeply in a cloud...felt himself being drawn back...deeply back to the present...BOOM BOOM BOOM and he was back—

Time travel was getting the right frequencies lined up, and time spent was random, but trips without something called a Dialer were minutes, sometimes seconds at best and strictly mind trips.

Using a Dialer according to Dr. Kublar was the real thing; a replica of you was physically there. The doctor promised to let him try this wondrous device one day. Eddie looked around at his small apartment. Baker was still blowing, then the tune ended. He made coffee, read more of his pages, noticed it was time to get ready if he was going to the Cabaret. He changed into a black velvet jacket, a white tux shirt and gray and black striped slacks. His Beatle boots needed a shine as well as new heels, so he wore a pair of gray suede semi-platforms he'd picked up in West Hollywood. When he went out he found the alley empty, quiet. He headed off through Chinatown toward North Beach and the Cabaret.

15

At the entrance stood a musclebound bouncer and a short guy wearing a flamboyant pullover that sparkled, a powder blue boa around his neck, full makeup, white hair, white eyebrows, a spiky shag. He recognized Eddie, maybe from his Wolf Snake connection and with a bright look said:

"Oh hello there. Pleased that you've come."

And to the bouncer "He gets in free, anytime."

A cute pixie girl appeared from behind the bouncer and stamped a green star on his hand.

Eddie walked down a semi-crowded hallway into a vast room with a sky high ceiling. A dance floor took up two thirds of the room. It was filled with people wearing their finest Glam gear grooving to the music amongst disco lights. "Bang A Gong" was playing loudly, and people were well into it. The bar, lounge area, pool tables, pinball machines took up the rest of the room. Eddie made his way through the crowd, getting some eye action from a couple cute glammed out girls. In the lounge area, he ordered a Cutty Sark and soda at the bar. He heard his name, and turned to see Richmond, Matt and Diamond Jack occupying a booth. Eddie joined them. He was pleased to see they were all still dressed in black. They discussed LA a bit, the finished record, and when the band would be playing next.

"The next gig is right here," said Matt. "...well, downstairs there's a club, and a sound system. It's beautiful and no one's using it. We met the owner earlier: He's a filthy rich screwball and a huge Glam rock fan who throws money around. He heard we're the hot ticket, so he asked us to play here."

Richmond said: "He questioned us about the all black thing, and made a snide remark asking if we were like bohemian artists. Jack growled at him: 'We're rockers mate. Black represents the death that we all face.' The owner got a worrisome look on his made up face and said: I see, but asked:

'Isn't this the glam and glitter revolution?'

'Black is all colors combined,' Matt said staring into his eyes until he caved and said:

'I get it guys. You're brilliant! Beautiful. Will you play here?'

Eddie laughed, said well done, and was noting the music selection: James Brown's "Payback," followed Jobriath's "Rock of Ages," and then Slade's "Come On Feel The Noise." When "Love Driver" came on cranked it seemed the whole place went crazy. The light man went overkill with the strobes. Afterward so many people were coming over to the booth to pay respect, smooze or give them drugs that Eddie slipped away. He noticed Sal Mineo of all people sitting with a younger man against a wall. They had been dancing and were all sweaty. The younger man went off somewhere, and Eddie introduced himself. He found Sal friendly and they chatted about his films and James Dean before the other guy came back. Eddie moved on. Some glam queen he'd met through another friend saw him, threw his arms around him, and began kissing him. Eddie politely pried him off; the guy shrugged, and threw himself back into the frantic dance crowd.

He spotted Beth with another man dressed badly as a woman. And then he saw a couple more, and that a whole group of men dressed badly as women had taken over a far corner. They were drinking cocktails, and laughing. Beth saw him, waved and called him over. Beth introduced him to Astrid, a short, olive skinned man with dark eyes and a silver wig. "Eddie, this place is very interesting. I can't thank you enough. But the loud music is a bit much for me, even with my earplugs." Astrid agreed, and snapped open a compact mirror, but only checked his teeth. Beth explained they were leaving soon to see Charles Pierce, a drag entertainer, perform nearby. In his ear Beth whispered that he'd had a breakthrough with the translation and was super excited. Eddie found the perfume these two wore overwhelming. It was like he was in some science fiction arboretum filled with the fumes of poisonous flower bombs. When they left he went over to where an industrial fan was blowing and stood there.

Alice was coming toward him like a vision as "Vicious" by Lou Reed was playing. He felt a jolt. His hormones were racing faster than the pulsing strobe lights. She was wearing a pink satin gown thats eccentric cut made her appear like a slightly mad, surreal goddess. Her eye shadow was streaked out almost to her hairline. She threw her arms around him and he held her. He felt her hand move down his back, circle his waist, arrive on his cock, and then settle under his balls. Her eyes gleamed, and he put his hand through a slit in her dress. He found her wearing nothing, and wet. He inserted his middle finger and she sighed. People were starting to notice them, so they moved to a back booth, but eventually left the club altogether and ended up in an unlocked car they found around the corner on Pacific.

***

Beth had a machine attached to the Tablet which was propped up. On a screen against the wall ancient script and symbols moved by. Beth made adjustments on a console. The screen went to snow, then swirls and then the text returned, but now in English. The words were not perfect, frequently misspelled, or fragmentations, but Beth could make them out, and took shorthand page by page. As the hours flew by he thought he might pass out. He had to pee.

He had to eat. He had drank all the beverages he'd gathered around him, but he couldn't stop. He was translating the history and philosophy of Lemuria, evidently written by a grand seer. It was a warning to future civilizations. Beth/Robert stopped translating before he lost consciousness. A while later he found himself drooling on the plush Oriental carpet. He crawled to a chair, pulled himself up, went into the bathroom. In the kitchen he gathered more drinks, snacks, and hurried back to the translation.

When he restarted the machine it now moved at a speed that he was comfortable with. Most curious he thought. Beth's wig was off, so the makeup, and earrings looked more bizarre. For a minute the realization of who he was and what he was doing moved through his brain like a soundless explosion. He kept transcribing madly. An hour later he took a shower, and an amphetamine, what his new friend Astrid called a black beauty. He went back to work. Six hours later, when the pill wore off, he finished. He felt as though he'd died and gone on to another world. Eventually his heart slowed down and he passed into a fitful sleep. He woke some time later to find Mu standing over him, talking to him. He offered him a hand, and said:

"Come, come Bet. You genius now. Doctor he reads it again. Reading now, this time, for you and me."

Beth let Mu lead him into the workroom where Dr. Kublar wearing a black velvet robe that perhaps some sorcerer king had worn in olden times, stood under the high domed window. The morning light illuminating him like a visitor from another world. The doctor spoke with resonance and mystery:

"War will eat your souls and then your world. It must be stopped. The Eaters of Light. The Eaters of Darkness. The warrior must know when. The people will let him know, not the so called holy men. The crystals of Akar must be kept, the sacred disc, the truth magic. I will teach the reader of this how to locate and save them from the twisted ones..."

The doctor looked at Beth and Mu. The screen was showing a picture of an idol that looked to have a South Pacific flavor, not a tiki exactly, but rather a melding of that style with something decidedly more intricate and Far Eastern, Hindu perhaps.

"Beth, you have surpassed any expectations. We are deeply in your debt."

"It was the most intense challenge I've ever faced. To say it was mind blowing would be a gross understatement. This is a wonder of the world and the messages the writer has conveyed from a time before time must be delivered to our leaders."

The doctor ruffled his sleeves, grunted, and stepped off a slight elevated section he'd been standing.

"You would think that would be the case. But do you really trust them? There is much information, so many techniques and rituals that in the wrong hands could be exploited for nefarious means."

"B-b-but doctor it's our government. If we can't trust them, then who? I insist we take this to them."

Mu began to stir slightly and cast a quick look at the doctor who made an audible click with his tongue. The doctor's eyes narrowed.

"Insist?"

"Yes, insist, as a citizen. I take an active interest in the political process, a bit of an activist really. I believe we are ultimately right. A lot of the world is under a satanic spell of evil and it's America's duty to crush that."

"Certainly you can see this is absolutist thinking, fanatical and false? Have you studied history? Even the drivel they teach in your schools can be deciphered well enough to show the irregularities to make a sharp mind look elsewhere for the real information and answers."

"B-b-but" Beth tried to interject. The doctor plowed ahead.

"Government is evil by its very nature. Oh there are a few

well intentioned men and women, but they're never given any real power. The system is simply too corrupt. The puppet masters would roar with laughter to hear of your unshakable belief in the system, although they would nod to your face and tell you you're being a good citizen. Do you watch TV news?"

"Well, of course I do, but I don't believe everything I hear."

"They don't expect you to, as long as the main messages get through. You've just shown that it has."

"Who do you work for Dr. Kublar?" Beth asked with a sudden accusing look which seemed to make Mu vibrate.

"We of the truth work for no one and everyone. Have you read Orwell?" Beth threw himself into a chair, ran a hand through his own reddish hair.

"Of course, in high school. But we live in a free society. Nothing like that could ever happen."

"What if I told you that in 35 years time when you go to the airport you will be sent through a radiation scanner that exposes you naked on a screen to government observers, and may include further action, like a molesting pat down, perhaps a strip search, or an anal probe? And how multiple radiation screenings can cause cancer? What if I told you that these scanners will be installed in train stations, bus stations, anywhere were there are crowds, and there will be roving street vans doing the same in the cities, and others in random highway stops? And what if I told you that you would not be allowed to leave the country if you owed taxes? What if I told you that the government could come into your home without a search warrant? Could wire tap you with no warrant? Would fill the skies with spy aircraft called drones? What if I told you the government could spy on each and every citizen? What if I told you that citizens could be arrested and held indefinitely without a lawyer, or even murdered anywhere in the world if the president decided that person was threat? And how would they define threat exactly? Remember how Big Brother twisted the meaning of words? Would you believe me if I showed you proof of all this?"

Beth looked up at him, his mouth hanging open. "Well, of course I'd believe it then, but the picture you paint is a nightmare. How could you possibly prove it?"

The doctor took off his cloak. Underneath, he was wearing a gray suit, and a black mock turtleneck. Doctor Kublar asked Mu to fetch what he called the Dialer. He explained to Beth it was a machine that would allow replicas of themselves to visit the future. Mu rose from a sitting position on the floor without the use of his hands. Beth watched as the strange contraption was wheeled out of a walk-in closet. It looked like an old radio from the fifties, he thought, but weirder, larger. And all those wires and tubes that circled it? The doctor approached it and blocked his view. From his arm movements, he looked to be making adjustments. Humming now, the Dialer was wheeled over. The doctor presented a needle on a cord connected to the Dialer. He explained it had to be inserted into Beth's leg. Another would be inserted into his own leg. He would be the guide and protector. Beth knew he was about to have a fantastic experience with this man. He was willing to take the risk, and nodded his approval.

Dr. Kublar sat on a stool next to him. The needles were inserted. At first Beth felt nothing and looked at the doctor as though he was engaged in something absurd. Then everything went fuzzy around the edges before a fluid blackness engulfed him. Beth felt a pull and saw streaks of light in his peripheral vision, then he was falling, falling, pleasantly, and he was excited about what he was falling into: Light. The doctor was next to him. Below was a bay and a ship: a flashing signal from someone onboard. They landed onto the deck like cats. Beth saw the city of San Francisco not far off. They were greeted by an older, slightly apish, robust man dressed in a naval uniform of sorts. He spoke to the doctor.

"We picked you up on the DWF, err the Dialer Wave Finder. Glad to be of service doctor. My boys will take you ashore. I have your control box." The man handed over a small black box that the doctor examined before putting into his pocket.

The Captain nodded, tipped his cap and was off. Beth thought he was not from this world but from another time, one ancient and ruled by magic.

"That's Elias," The doctor said. "At a later date I will tell you his legend and significance. It's monumental." A young man came around the corner dressed in gray work clothes. He was joined by another man a few years older dressed similarly except for a black leather vest and a watch cap.

"Hi there," the first one said, introducing himself as Jamie, and the other jokingly as "the private eye". They busied themselves lowering a motor boat boat, and securing a ladder for them to descend into it. Once settled the private eye pushed the boat off and started the motor. They headed to shore. At the dock Jamie went over how to use the box with the doctor, showing him how it doubled as an electronic map. Beth was still awestruck, and hung onto the doctor as they made their way along the Embarcadero. The doctor saw a Yellow Cab, hailed it.

"The cars are amazing! People are talking on hand held phones like Star Trek!" Beth exclaimed, staring wide eyed out the window as the taxi moved through the city streets. They ended up at a cyber café South of Market where the doctor pointed out the newspapers at a stand. Beth saw the headlines first: President Obama signs NDAA: Indefinite Detention of US citizens Bill. Beth saw that the date was January 1st 2012. He read the first page and said: "Good grief!" He held the paper shaking slightly. He looked at the doctor like a child might look at his parents after some fantastic mystery was explained.

"Come inside," the doctor said softly. "This is called a cyber café. Most people have their own computers, but these cafés are still popular with students, some travelers too."

They sat at one and after only a few minutes of instruction from the doctor Beth was flying around the internet scanning stories, and speed reading pages of news from varied sources. The doctor gave him headphones, and he watched and listened to video clips as well. A while later Beth handed the earphones back, shut the computer down, turned to the doctor and said:

"Good freakin' lord! You're right. We must never give these bastards anything, ever!"

The doctor took out the black box, programmed it, and pressed a button. A golden light formed around them. The light pulsed and looked to be ready to explode. A loud POP and everything went black again, but this time Beth was having trouble breathing. He lost consciousness and came to with Mu flicking water on his face. He was still breathing hard, experiencing vertigo. The doctor approached with a vial with vapor rising from it. He instructed Beth to drink it quickly. He did and immediately felt like his old self. The needles had been removed, the Dialer put away. Blood was trickling from his nose which Mu dabbed with a tissue.

"Nothing to be concerned with," said Dr. Kublar patting his hand. "In high altitude pressure areas a slight epistaxi can occur from a minor anterior burst. A wet tissue ball will fix it up nicely, like corking a bottle of wine."

16

Eddie met Alice downtown in Union Square at the appointed time. They arrived at exactly the same moment and laughed at the coincidence. Eddie suggested a drink and they walked over to Lefty O'Douls. Since the place was almost empty they took a booth.

"What movie are we seeing" Alice asked tasting her gin and tonic.

"Actually two films if you're up for it. Yakuza films from Japan, one of my latest interests."

Alice screwed up her face a little so Eddie elaborated. "Japanese gangsters in secret crime societies who get elaborate tattoos, chop their fingers off if they commit an offense, and see themselves upholding Samurai warrior creed. These two are black and white with English subtitles. Asian film noir, really."

"Sounds groovy and strange. Where?"

"Japantown. We take the 38 Geary. We'll cab back. Where do you live by the way?"

"I've taken Maggie's place for the summer. She's in Spain. After that I don't know. I may move to southern California."

Eddie told her about his visit there with Wolf Snake, and his impressions of LA. She asked him if he could live there. He was ambiguous: "Well, not anytime soon. I'm studying under a special teacher, and working on a novel of sorts."

Alice smiled slightly: "You're an interesting guy, Eddie". She stroked his face across the table. He kissed her hand. They caught a bus and arrived in Japantown in an upbeat mood. Alice insisted on smoking a joint around the back of the Peace Pagoda. They wandered around the mall, shortly becoming absorbed with the photography and art books in the Kinokuniya Bookstore. They found the lighting harsh, so they put on sunglasses. They left the mall, crossed the street, and entered the theater right on time, although only a handful of people were in attendance.

The first film was excellent and blew them both away. More people showed up for the second one which Eddie found slower, and not nearly as compelling. He was wondering why the director had chosen the pacing when he felt Alice's hand on his leg. She dropped her jacket over her hand, unbuckled and unzipped his pants. Alice wrapped her hand around his prick. She withdrew her hand, and wetted it with saliva. She gave him various levels of pleasure until finally, in a rapid motion brought him to orgasm. She had Kleenex for him too. He was laughing as he cleaned up, zipped up, and kissed her tenderly. People around them were grunting, and shushing them, so they straightened up. They watched the end of the film. Alice propped her legs on the back of the empty seat in front of her, and continued to snicker a little. Leaving the theater Alice held his arm, and said: "Even the second one was a lot more interesting than most modern Hollywood movies. I love foreign films."

Eddie said that he would always remember that one fondly. She laughed, and squeezed his arm. They decided that the night was young and were both up for a to visit the Cabaret even though it was a week night. Eddie flagged a Yellow Cab that delivered them to Broadway and Montgomery. It looked to be a quiet night in North Beach. They were waved into the club, since they were both on the never pay list. But once inside were greeted by a room maybe only a third full. They decided that was a good thing. They could relax, be themselves, and take a whole booth. There were fewer people to bother them, and they would have plenty of room on the dance floor. They tossed their jackets into a booth, and settled in with cocktails. Alice put her legs up and Eddie started getting aroused again. "Do The Strand" by Roxy Music came on, one of Alice's favorites. She insisted they dance. They were both good dancers, measuring each other the way dancers do.

When the tune segued into James Brown's "Papa Don't Take No Mess" Eddie was impressed with her moves and kept his subtle, and steady. They danced well together. Someone called Alice by name. Across the dance floor was a cluster of dancers gyrating, and shimmying; a flamboyant, androgynous male was dancing wildly and waving. Alice waved back. Eddie noticed that the guy's tongue was hanging out and he commented on that. Alice looked again, laughed, said he was on something for sure. She called him Danny The Dancer and he was proving that by doing incredible spins and splits. Eddie half expected him to do a flip. Suddenly, he didn't feel like such the great dancer himself. Alice took his mind off that when she fell into his arms for a slow dance to Sinatra singing Cole Porter's "What Is This Thing Called Love?"

Later Eddie played pinball, enjoying it since usually you had to sign up on a waiting list to play. When he finally gave it up he turned it over to a kid who looked too young to be in a bar legally. He had a thin pimply face, and wore an exaggerated quiff of jet black hair, leather jacket, white T shirt, toothpick clamped in-between bad teeth, and an eager look in his eye regarding the machine. Eddie headed over to their booth expecting to find Alice chatting with a friend or two. Instead, she was at the bar, on a high barstool. She was sitting next to another girl with raven hair, and a ponytail. They were making out. Eddie didn't know what to think at first except: bisexual: well, that was different, kind of a turn on actually. He figured he would play it cool, and hang out in the booth with his drink.

Some tourists sitting in an upper section stared at them making out, commenting to each other until Danny the Dancer, and an older drag queen took a table near them. Danny and his friend were laughing loudly, and shrieking over some private joke or gossip. This caused the little pack of tourists to get up, and head for the exit. Eddie laughed. On cue Alice turned around, smiled, hopped off the barstool. The other girl briefly turned around too, and Eddie saw she was a fox. But only Alice joined him in the booth. She took out a fan she had bought in Japantown, began fanning herself.

"Whose your friend?"

"Wouldn't you like to know?"

"Sure, why not?"

"Did you like what you saw?"

"Sure, groovy."

Alice threw down her fan. "That was a goof man, a prank to freak out the tourists and make them leave."

"I see, but they were as intrigued as I was. Really, it was the screeching of Danny the Dancer and his friend that did the trick."

Alice looked over at them. They were still laughing, and carrying on. Danny suddenly stood, shimmied, and let out a shrill whistle. Alice frowned.

"I see, well, we've done it before with very good results let me tell you."

"Cool. Can I get you another drink?"

Alice, now in a crap mood, turned down the drink, and said that really she should be getting home because she had to work in the morning. Eddie asked if he could see her home or get her a cab.

"Eddie, I can take care of myself already. Don't be so serious."

"Alice, I had a terrific time tonight. I'm sorry you're upset."

She stood, sighed, said she wasn't upset and headed for the exit. Eddie was feeling angry and confused when he looked up to see the pony tail standing above him with a sexy, sassy look on her beauty queen face. She was wearing a low cut evening dress that sparkled here and there as if communicating with the diamond sparkles on her earlobes. She was holding a glass of sparkling champagne.

"Hi I'm Amanda, Alice's friend?"

"Hi, Eddie," he said, and stood, motioning for her to join him in the booth.

"Did you enjoy our little show?'

"I did but I don't think Alice enjoyed the fact that I did."

Amanda laughed, a throaty laugh that seemed to affect her whole body. She gave him an inviting look with a hint of a smile.

"Sorry Eddie, I couldn't help myself. Sometimes Alice is a little too clever for her own good. I like that you enjoyed it. Have you ever been with two girls at the same time?"

"Have you? Guys that is? ...or girls for that matter," Eddie countered with a grin, thinking that Amanda was even wilder than Alice.

"Asked you first," she said and he felt her shoeless foot under the table climbing his leg to rest on his prick. His partial erection stiffened. Eddie was looking at her mouth, wanting to kiss her.

"Eddie, come home with me. I live nearby. It's kismet or something. Come on."

He didn't hesitate, and both the owner and bouncer gave them knowing looks as they made their way out.

"Drama at the Cabaret. It's a fucking Peyton Place. Don't let it bore you Eddie."

He was fascinated with Amanda. Her apartment on the 17th floor overlooked the bay, COIT Tower and Alcatraz. Amanda went off to the bathroom. A little later she came back, naked but for a long peacock blue boa. It trailed behind her as she sashayed off toward the open bedroom. Eddie began taking off his clothes, as he followed after her. In bed he admitted that he had been with two chicks at once. Amanda said that she was equal to any two bitches around. He laughed and laid back as if to say: go ahead, prove it. She climbed on top, covered his face with a hand which he licked, and then the fun began.

Breakfast with Amanda was not what Eddie was expecting. She was a lawyer, who worked in the financial district. She sat across from him wearing a pin striped business suit. She looked at him through studious glasses. Matter of factly she explained that she was two different people, literally day and night. They left the apartment complex together. Eddie felt more like her client than her lover. He thought that it was probably mutual, since it was a one night stand. But maybe more nights would be involved since they were both habitués of the Cabaret, and were good together in bed. When they parted ways Amanda kissed him on the cheek, and walked off. He admired her legs in high heels, the most sexy part of her daytime persona. He was always glad to return to Chinatown. He felt his apartment there was a safe haven as well as a place for learning and working. He stopped to look in a store window at a display of jade jewelry. Chinese new Year was coming soon:

The Year of The Tiger.

17

Beth was coming out of the building as Eddie headed in. Beth was dressed as a man, sans wig, makeup. Eddie didn't recognize him at first.

"Eddie! Come with me for a coffee? I have something exciting to tell you."

"Hi—can you wait a minute? Actually, I have some coffee from Café Trieste at my place, and I really need to take a piss. Can you um come up?"

"Sure. Sure. That's probably better too." Beth was acting anxious, and Eddie wondered what was up. As they climbed the stairway Beth, behind, said, "Hey Eddie do me a favor and address me as Robert when I'm like this. Okay?"

"You bet," Eddie said, loud enough for Robert to hear and unlocked his apartment door. He flipped a light switch, went over to the window and opened the blind to let in light. He went back and flipped the light switch off again, as Robert watched. Eddie gestured to the semi-comfortable chair that Mu had brought down one day since the other was just a basic wooden number. Robert took it and lit a cigarette.

"Un momento, and I'll make some coffee." Eddie headed for the bathroom. Robert picked up and flipped through a glossy magazine on Japanese cinema and scanned an article about classic Samurai films. Eddie came back out, but before he could make coffee Robert said:

"Dr. Kublar has given me permission to share with you something I've experienced with him that has shaken my belief in everything I previously thought was real and believed in. Do you realize the greatness of Kublar?"

"I think I do, but please go on."

"I've broken the code. I've translated the Tablet. The writer was a high seer in the fabled, yet it turns out very real world of Lemuria, a place that, like Atlantis, I never believed existed. The revelations are breathtaking, and mind shattering. This is big Eddie. Way beyond what I thought was remotely possible except in fantastic fiction or sci fi movies."

"Do tell."

Robert told Eddie of the experience and elaborated with each question posed. Eddie had his own time travel experiences, red light guardian visitations, and other mind altering sessions, so this wasn't quite as mind bending. Eddie shared some of this too with Robert since he'd been accepted into the family—a family far reaching even through time. Then a kind of realization/recognition came over Eddie as he spoke. He felt like he was peaking on acid. Robert too looked hyper-alert, and fanatical. A light tap at the door brought them back. Robert had jumped but Eddie calmed him: "It's Mu."

"Ah Mister Edward, Mister Robert, the Magus, er Dr. Kublar would like your presence at great meeting. Come prease."

They followed him upstairs into the living room where they took seats. Dr. Kublar entered wearing a striped Moroccan djellaba, and remained standing.

"Gentlemen a new dawn is breaking, but also a new war. We've been betrayed by an agent of the enemy: The Ugly Ones. Agents and assassins have been dispatched, but we're ahead simply by having this information. Once the Tablet is safely installed in the power cave along with the crystals of Akar, the sacred disc, and the truth magic, it will be safe, and never accessible to them. But, they know this. They know it is here. They are on their way."

The doctor clicked his tongue, and for the first time Eddie saw a wave of anger cross his face.

"Since it has arrived in this time, this time it must remain. I cannot take it into the past nor into the future. We can however take it to an alternative, or parallel world. It must be protected. Mu will appear to have the Tablet when they do arrive, and take them on a wild goose chase. Edward will have already taken it to Mexico City D.F. where he will remain for the placement ceremony."

"I've always wanted to go to Mexico," Robert blurted out perhaps hoping to join Eddie, but the doctor said:

"And to Mexico you shall go, but for a different assignment and not for another month or so."

"You tell me when. I'm ready," said Eddie. In Robert's mind a suspended moon had begun to spin, at a medium speed at first, then so fast to be a blur of white flashes causing him to topple over. The doctor was at his side. Mu appeared from the shadows, gave him an injection. Robert sat back up with a confused look. The doctor said:

"You still need rest. I want you to recuperate in your room, and I will attend to you for another twenty four hours." Dr. Kublar turned to Eddie:

"You leave in one hour. All arrangements have been made. I wish we had more time for training, but we don't. I have contacts in the capitol so the most dangerous part is your time here, and your return, which Mu will instruct you about on the way. We have a slight advantage. We know they are coming. Pack quickly. Mu will drive you to the airport."

When Mu pulled the old Buick onto the freeway, he kept looking in his rearview mirror. Eddie wondered if they were onto them. Would they kill him, and Mu, or just take the Tablet that

Eddie had in a bag of camera equipment? His cover was as a photographer doing a book on Mexico City, the publisher: Kublar Inc., and an official looking to-whom-it-may-concern letter to that effect. Eddie found the cover story interesting since he had recently been experimenting more with photography as an aid to his writing. Mu gave him a report, and how-to instructions to deal with his certain interrogation and confinement on the return trip. Eddie wasn't thrilled about that news. Mu steered the Buick onto Airport Drive, and pulled up to Mexicana Airlines departing terminal.

"Stay seated prease." They sat there for what seemed a long time before Mu said: "Okay, we go now."

Mu insisted on carrying his bag, and staying with him as he checked in. He only left when Eddie was headed for the security checkpoint to go to his gate.

In Mexico City Eddie checked into a hotel on Avenue Reforma across from a park. The smells in the air were completely different to him. It was exciting, this being his first time out of the country. He felt because of the doctor's tip off, and the quick move to send him off, he was safe. Still he would feel better once the Tablet was settled in the cave. Again under his belt, he carried the magical artifact, afraid his shoulder bag could be swiped. Taking a walk, he remembered the Aliester Crowley story of when the black magician had visited the capitol: he'd been out walking along with somebody, when Crowley decided to follow some old man. Crowley began imitating his walk, then purposely tripped, and the man he was mimicking tripped as well.

Eddie carefully watched to see to see if anyone was following him. He felt confident enough, but kept himself in the moment, aware of his surroundings, and on the watch for anyone who might appear too friendly. Dr. Kublar had taught him to act as if he knew exactly what he was doing, regardless of how he felt.

He walked through the park where a number of young lovers

were occupying benches, heads together, smooching. He came across a theater. At the box office window he found a Mexican woman wearing a black shawl, dozing, leaning against the wall in the small booth. She sensed him, and snapped her eyes open. "Si Señor?" Eddie bought a ticket for the Ballet Folkloric. The doctor had given him a list of places to visit, and things to do. The ballet was on the list. He took a cab to the Pink Zone that catered to tourists and wandered around there until he found a restaurant that looked inviting. He took a small outside table. He listened to a strolling Marachi group who had stopped. They were dressed in glitzy finery and impressive sombreros. He tipped them along with some other tourists who had gathered to listen. Later, back at the hotel, he found the massive front doors locked. He rang the bell, then again, and again, becoming irritated. A humped over bald little man appeared. He was wearing a waiter's uniform, and had a towel draped over his arm. He explained the lockup in Spanish which Eddie couldn't understand. Once he conveyed that that he didn't speak Espanol the man said: "Banditos!" He made his hand like a gun, scowled, winked, turned and ambled away. Eddie found his bed comfortable, and the place deliciously quiet. He had read a brochure earlier. The hotel had once been a monastery. He drifted off thinking about one señorita in particular he'd seen strutting about in the pink zone.

18

Early the next day Eddie set out full of excitement and curiosity. He continued to carry the Tablet under his belt, snug to his lower back. He would follow his instincts and do a little exploring. He boarded a colectivo on the hotel man's instructions. When he got out he dropped what he thought was the correct fare into the driver's cup. The driver laughed, shook his head and pulled away.

Eddie got out a little later since across the street he saw a magnificent cathedral surrounded by gardens and palm trees. It looked more like a kingdom, he thought. Young men were gardening the grounds. They wore wide brim straw hats, loose white shirts and linen pants. An older man with a bushy mustache approached and offered him an Aztec rug. Eddie liked it, but didn't want burdened at the start of the day's adventure. He walked along a tree lined street, then through an alleyway by orche colored buildings with peeling paint and washing hanging from the windows. A group of squealing children ran by chasing a boy whose red kite trailed a few feet above.

Eddie came to a square with a few shoe shine stands. The stands had canvas canopies for protection from the sun. It was morning, but already the heat could be felt. Nearby a woman sold flowers. At another stand corn on the cob was being turned over on a grill. Another vendor used the top of a trash can to display a cardboard box filled with syrupy yams. Across the street stood a light gold painted house with white lattice work around the windows. The colors here stood out to Eddie as if he'd only just realized the power of color. Across the way a new vendor was setting up grotesque posters of Jesus on the cross. But there was a benign one too of Him in heaven bathed in supernatural light.

Eddie found his way to Chapultepec Park. He admired the grounds from a vantage point, with the lake shimmering in the early light. Here the Aztecs had once ruled. He imagined such a world. He walked up to the Museo Nacional Antropologia, and took at look at the Castillo de Chapultepec. Later he passed by the neighborhood of Coyocan and saw another stunning cathedral. He visited Frida Kahlo's blue house. After a meal of cheese filled nopal that he learned were cactus, along with rice, beans, all eaten in a blue plastic tent of a place, he took a cab back. He found his room made up, pulled off his boots and took a siesta. A violin played a melancholy sleepy serenade somewhere outside.

Later he visited the main zocala which he'd passed the first evening. The tricolor flag of Mexico flew everywhere. A huge one stood in the middle of the square. He was just in time to see the army marching in and filling half the plaza. They began to execute impressive precision march maneuvers in front of the National Palace. People cheered and clapped, as they marched out.

Eddie approached a driver who was parked nearby. He found that he spoke some English. He was friendly with smiling eyes, and a thick mustache. Eddie explained that he wanted to visit a certain wax museum. The driver had never heard of the place. Eddie pulled out his notebook, and showed him the address. "Ahh, Si Señor." Eddie then negotiated a fare that sounded reasonable.

When they arrived Eddie asked him not to wait, so the driver wrote down his phone number, and told him he was available for day tours or excursions.

Eddie found two twin older women wearing black shawls similar to the teller at the Ballet Folkloric booth, except these two had prominent moles above their left eyes. He paid thirty pesos and began the tour. He felt like he was the only one in the place. The renderings were bad as expected, but amusing to Eddie, especially a replica of Frank Sinatra that looked more like a giant action figure, soulless and plastic, yet haunted. Eddie took a photograph. The Elvis wax figure looked more like Koloth, the Klingon captain sans the beard. Behind Elvis were three men extending their right arms. Eddie couldn't figure out who they were supposed to be. Maybe the Jordanaires? Two of them looked like waiters though, and the third wore a white suit. The one in white stepped forward, Eddie jumped.

"Sorry to startle you," the man said with a laugh. "I'm Pipeto, your contact."

"How did you—?"

"I followed you, and I had to wait for the right place and time, This was beautiful, but why did you want to see this? This is not the wax museum tourists go to."

"A friend recommended it, not because it's good, but because it's so bad."

Pipeto looked a little confused, and took Eddie by the arm. "Well, are you done here? I can take you to the cave, and you can place the Tablet. Then we can all sleep better."

They went out a back entrance that Pipeto located near the bathrooms. They walked down a tree lined street. They climbed in the car Pipeto pointed out, a two tone blue late sixties Chevy Impala. Street scenes passed by, reflected on the glass in a backwards blur as Eddie looked out. A short time later Pipeto pulled up and stopped before a wide garage door in a prosperous looking neighborhood. In a moment the door opened and they entered. The car's headlights came on and they rolled in. The garage door shut behind them. They drove down a ramp and entered a long tunnel. On the other end they came out under an overcast sky. They traveled down a country road with avocado trees to one side, and llamas staring dumbly at them on the other side. They entered a wooded area where there were no signs of life. The trees were dead, gray, and ghostly.

"Dead forest," Pipeto said. "No sounds."

After twenty minutes or so they approached a bridge that traversed a wide gray sluggish river. There was still no life anywhere. Pipeto turned to Eddie, but Eddie said: "Dead river?" Pipeto smiled: "Si Señor."

On the other side Eddie was delighted to see the sun come out in all its glory, to a living, breathing jungle of palmettos, and mangroves, filled with birds and animals calls. Then he saw more. Chattering monkeys leaped from tree to tree. Huge butterflies floated by. A wild cat looked at them rather serenely from behind a clump of jungle foliage. Pipeto drove at a crawl so he could enjoy it all. Eddie felt wonderful. It was like the feeling of well being good acid can deliver; a sense of oneness with the universe and all that. He felt perhaps Pipeto had taken him to a new Eden, an enchanted land where mythical creatures could appear at any moment.

Pipeto parked to the side of a dirt road. By foot they began climbing, soon seeing spectacular views of deserts, mountain ranges, and clouds well below them. "Like la Zona del Silencio but different," Pepito said stopping for a minute, wiping his brow with a handkerchief. They made their way past a lovely, impressive waterfall. Eddie thought a swim in the natural pool at the bottom would be delightful. They continued to climb a worn path. At the top they were sweating, and breathing heavily. They looked out over a circular valley, filled with moss, surrounded by craggy mountains the color of bone and pockmarked with cave entrances of all sizes. They made their way down on a worn rope ladder. Eddie felt giddy for a minute, then a new strength gripped him.

When he stepped onto terra firma he heard the humming of voices.

Out of the caves came a procession of small people who lined up before them. They looked to be Indians with wise, old faces and eyes that sparkled like crystal. They wore buckskin and indigo necklaces that generated a kind of energy Eddie could feel. Pipeto spoke to them in a language that was not Spanish. They stopped humming and listened. "Show them the Tablet," he said to Eddie who removed it from his pack. Intuitively he held it above his head like a latter day Moses. The little people fell to their knees and in unison began to sing a curious refrain that touched Eddie in a way that no other music ever had. The little people stood and their leader or spokesman who looked much younger stepped forward. He spoke to Eddie in English:

"The Tablet will be safe now, at home with the crystals of Akar, the sacred disc, and the truth magic. You are most brave, and you will be remembered here forever. Please follow us now."

Eddie and Pipeto followed the small army into one of the larger caves that was meagerly lit by the torches the little people picked up at the entrance. After walking deep into the cave for what seemed a long time they stopped in front of a massive wooden door that must have been built by an extinct race of giants. The leader climbed a ladder, and turned the lock with both hands. He climbed down and the small army pushed the door open. They crowded into an area that Eddie quickly realized was a platform descending on a rope pulley system. As seconds passed Eddie wondered about the air supply, but then they stopped, another massive door opened the same way. They entered a huge chamber with no ceiling in sight, only a kind of blur high above.

The holy place had a spectacular altar at one end that looked to have been dipped in gold. Multiple baroque sub-altars and statues encrusted in splendid jewels lined the rest of the room.

The little people kneeled, Pipeto did as well, and pulled Eddie down. A red light from a round compartment was generating at the main altar. The light grew, and like a searchlight stretched out and fell upon Eddie. He rose holding the Tablet above his head again. The little people looked at each other curiously, shrugged, and began a soft hum. He approached the altar. The round tabernacle opened. A golden box slid out. Eddie placed the Tablet in it. The tabernacle retracted with the box and closed. Eddie felt a profound release. The room filled with swirling lights. The little people began levitating one by one, and disappearing into the gloom above. Only Eddie, Pipeto and the leader remained. The leader, whose eyes were red pinpoints, now began to levitate too. He waved a tiny hand in front of their eyes and everything went black.

Eddie and Pipeto found themselves back at the waterfall. They watched the little people who'd brought them there on stretchers scramble away, and disappear back into the jungle. Eddie began to undress for a swim. Pipeto sat up, and smoked a hand rolled cigarette.

Eddie was charged, and elevated to another level of vitality. On the drive back Pipeto took a different route to pass the pyramids of the sun and the moon. They stopped a ways off and admired them in silence.

He wrote in his notebook until he grew tired enough to sleep. The following day he decided to skip a visit to Xochimilco's floating gardens, and instead attended a Luche libra exhibition in an old bull ring. That night he took in the Ballet Folkloric, and the following morning he caught a flight to Acapulco for two days in the sun before his return. He realized with a bad feeling that the hard part of the mission was still ahead of him. But, really, he reasoned, how hard could it be?

19

He stood in line at LAX to go through immigration. He had his form ready. He had listed his small purchases, and filled out his tourist visa as well. The line, one of two, was moving slowly. He was tempted to switch to the other that was moving faster when two airport security cops approached him. One, Hispanic, looked aggressive. The other, a older, fat white guy, came off more low key.

"You Edward Knox?" the older guy asked, and Eddie's heart felt like it had dropped to his feet. He adjusted to the moment. A small part of him hoped it was some anomaly or another, but he knew better.

"Yes, what's the problem?"

"Come with us sir."

They had Eddie walk between them, and he continued to ask what the problem was. The fat one said out the side of his mouth:

"You're being detained by the FBI. That's all we know."

"This is it," Eddie thought as he was escorted down an off white stairway, up a slightly inclining hallway, down two industrial gray hallways, and finally directed into a room that held a desk, two chairs, and nothing else. There was nothing on the walls or even a wastepaper basket in sight, no window. The door was shut, and the older fat cop sat down at the desk. The young Hispanic leaned against a wall. Eddie went to sit down and the younger man barked:

"Empty your pockets bitch, remove your belt, shoes, jewelry and put your bag on the desk."

Eddie complied as the younger one reached over, and took the chair. He sat in it backwards, and looked at Eddie in a menacing manner, showing the glint of a gold tooth. The older guy looked through his stuff, and deadpan said:

"We have to search you thoroughly. You're on a list. Sorry. I'm going to have to ask you to take off your clothes now." The younger guy snickered. The older guy told him to be cool.

"Ifanititifanbidit" Eddie repeated internally. The red light flooded him and there was a humming in his head. He looked at his captors almost serenely. He was glad the older man was there to prevent the cavity search from being abusive since then he would have to kill them like Dr. Kublar had taught him to do. He knew he was getting an ass check, it was part of the intimidation the doctor had warned him about. If the older man wasn't there he would probably have to kill the other guard and escape, wearing his uniform, he thought. In actuality once Eddie had heard the complete assignment from Dr. Kublar he wasn't as enthused as he had been initially, but he trusted the doctor. He had been instructed to follow the procedures and to admit to everything, but to deny that he knew the government was involved or had any interest in the ancient head.

The ass search administered by the younger man wearing surgical gloves was nothing much, since his superior observed, but when Eddie started to get dressed he was stopped. The fat one pulled out a green plastic jumpsuit from a desk drawer, handed it to him. Once in it he was handcuffed, led out of the room down the hallway into another larger room. He was uncuffed, told to strip again. He was pointed to what looked like a shower area where a half dozen people could stand. But there was no shower heads, just a long drain. In the soap dish were plastic packets. He was instructed to open one, and cover his body with the gel. He was left to stand there when the fat one closed a drab curtain. He stood there feeling the goop, and sensing a little sting from it, when the curtain reopened. There stood his captors, but the Hispanic thug had a hose that trailed into another room. He held it with both hands, a cruel look in his eyes. He turned on the nozzle, and did his best to humiliate him with the intense jet spray that shot out. He commanded him to turn around, and bend over. Eddie, though, was protected by the red light. He was in a state where it didn't bother him. This frustrated the sadist. Eventually the fat one said: "That's enough Juan." Juan reluctantly shut it off. He complained about it in Spanish, and said "fucker," as he dragged the hose away.

Eddie was given a thin towel and his underwear and a new jumpsuit by the older, sane guy. This jumpsuit was made of stiff material that was a little uncomfortable, but better than the plastic one. At least the disinfectant gel was removed from his skin. They took him back down the hallway, onto a grungy elevator and went up. They arrived on a floor that was on obvious lock down: a row of gray steel cells on either side. He was put in one of the last ones, and locked in. He looked around: cot, brown blanket, sink, commode: What luxury he thought, and laughed.

A few hours later a tray of food was given to him through a slot in the door: rubbery looking meat loaf, peas, watery mashed potatoes, and a piece of white bread. Eddie wasn't hungry, and ignored it. A while later it was taken back. A bottle of water appeared; he drank half of that. The bed sheet had the stink of bleach so he covered it with the blanket. He eventually fell to sleep still wearing the jumpsuit. He slept fitfully on his back, and was awake an hour later when the door opened. There stood two goons in full riot gear including face guards. Eddie knew this tactic was to unnerve him, to intimidate him more, and soften him for the inevitable interrogation. They handcuffed him, blindfolded him, dragged him down the hallway. They pushed him into another room. He hit a wall, and almost fell. He tried to prepare for the coming blows as best he could, but they didn't come. Instead a voice did:

"Jackson, uncuff this citizen and remove that blindfold. What's with you people anyway?"

Across the room, Eddie saw two chairs facing each other. A man in a black suit sat in one smoking a cigarette. Jackson, still standing next to Eddie, was a black man who looked like a linebacker, whose expression said that he was a mindless killing machine. He folded his arms. The man in the suit said:

"Mr. Knox, please join me over here. Pay no ill will to Jackson, he was just following protocol. For some reason, a glitch really is why you were placed on a high alert/danger list. We simply wanted a friendly word with you." The man unfolded a piece of paper, and looked at it. "Jackson, I have the clearance form, and an explanation of the fuck up here. You can leave us now."

Jackson said yes sir, turned, and left the room. Eddie stepped over and took a seat as instructed. The interrogator was an unlikely candidate or so Eddie thought. He wasn't much older than himself, with a thin, boney face. He wore round glasses, a black tight fitting suit, white shirt, and a skinny tie. He extended an almost skeletal hand.

"Agent Sheldon," he said, offering a weak smile. Eddie shook his surprisingly firm hand, and remained quiet. He remembered Dr. Kublar's instructions: Don't talk when you don't have to. Answer the questions, but keep your answers brief.

"So, Mr. Knox. May I call you Eddie? Good. I know you're not a dangerous criminal, but you know where a certain artifact is that the government needs to find, especially to stop it from getting into the wrong hands. Do you know what I'm referring to?"

"If you mean the Tablet, on Dr. Kublar's instructions I delivered it to Mexico City D.F., and placed it in a power cave. He said it was valuable, but I had no idea that the government would be interested in an ancient artifact."

Agent Sheldon scoffed.

"Where exactly did you deliver it to?"

Eddie told him the story while Sheldon listened, said hm-mm, and at the end said good lord. Agent Sheldon stared at Eddie with his mouth slightly open.

"Would you submit to a polygraph?"

"Sure, why not? Everything I've told you is the truth."

Sheldon looked at his wristwatch, made a little sucking sound as though he had something caught in his teeth, and said:

"Okay, I'll set one up. Sorry, but you'll have to remain in custody until we get the results."

Later that day Eddie was moved out a back entrance, down some metal stairways with five other prisoners. They were loaded onto a security van. They were driven for what seemed the better part of an hour. They arrived at a grim prison set on the grounds in the center of a dusty valley. He was finger printed, and issued a new uniform: gray cotton slacks, a long sleeve matching shirt, and shoes similar to Chinese slippers. He was escorted down a wide hallway that was rather quiet. He was given a cell that wasn't much different than the one he'd been in, except there was a high, barred window. If he stood on his cot, in the distance he could see part of a field, some haggard trees, and the road they had come in on. The guard had left the cell open. He wandered out for a look around. There were a dozen cells in the section: D Block. The day room held chairs, tables, and a TV mounted high on the wall in its own little cage. He would learn the TV was on for one hour viewing after dinner. The prisoners voted on what to watch. He went into the day room, and found some of his new neighbors. They were a sketchy, brutal looking bunch sitting around drinking out of styrofoam cups, playing checkers, talking, reading, and watching the main hallway for any traffic.

Eddie took an old issue of Time from a stack of magazines, and tried to keep to himself in a corner. But all eyes were on him. Eventually one brute stepped over, loomed over him, and said: "Ain't you a purty thang," then asked him who the fuck he was, and why the fuck he was here. Eddie had been instructed by the doctor on how to deal with this kind of situation. He swiftly kicked the man in the testicles. The others turned, and blocked the view so a passing guard would not see. Eddie pounded the man's face with lightening fists. His agile fingers jabbed and pressed his pain centers. One last solid right jab and the man crumbled to the floor. Eddie looked at his work, said to him:

"The name is Eddie Knox, and I hope I've taught you some manners today." He went back to his magazine as two of the beaten man's cohorts helped him back to his cell. There were murmurs, and whispers that Eddie wished he could hear. He felt someone new standing over him, who then sat beside him.

"Max Griffin," the huge black man said, offering a meaty hand. Eddie gave it a shake, saw his own bloody knuckles.

"You look like Levi Stubbs from The Four Tops," Eddie said.

"Now how does a white boy know the names of the Four Tops?"

"I'm a music lover and in my teenage years the music was rhythm and blues, or soul music." Eddie rattled off the records he had listened to, the acts he had seen. Max said my my, laughed like he could hardly believe some of the artists Eddie was so familiar with. Eddie told him that he had seen Solomon Burke in Harrisburg at a certain venue and Max said:

"Wait a minute. I was at that show. It was all brothers. You is either brave or crazy or both."

"A little of both I guess when it comes to music, but I'll tell you this: music unites. I never had a spot of trouble when I've attended those mostly black clubs, but I also had some black friends who'd sometimes come along."

Max and Eddie continued to discuss rhythm and blues, then straight up blues. Each amazed one another on their knowledge and experiences. Eventually Max spoke lower and said:

"That animal you laid out is Gutz. He used to have a big ass belly, but he lost the weight in here. He's a dangerous fuck. He has a small but loyal gang, and you've just become his number one enemy. The guards in this section aren't bad, but they can't be around all of the time. I'll keep an eye out too."

"Thanks."

Eddie slept through TV hour although he occasionally woke, to hear the men hooting, and clapping over the sound. He opted to stay in his cell even though he would be locked in for the night. He was pleased with that rule since it meant Gutz and his pals couldn't attack him in his sleep.

He was woken at 5 AM with a guard opening his cell and saying: "Wash and dress. Chow in fifteen."

D Block lined up and were inspected by two guards. The gate was unlocked, and like school children they were marched down the hallway in single file. The chow room was a vast sea of gray shirts and quiet as a church, except for the squeaking of chairs and men slurping tea, occasional coughs, sneezes, and obscene clearings of their throats. Guards were everywhere, closely watching the cons eat. Eddie's line approached the food dispensary where a fat white woman, and a fat black man wearing splattered aprons and dilapidated chef hats looked at them dully. A skinny white guy in need of a shave at the end poured tea into tin cups. Eddie was starving and the crappy fare looked good. When the woman asked if he'd like more of a stewed apple dish he said yes ma'am, and thanked her. She smiled, and gave him a plump portion.

At the table he ate quickly, but methodically. When he finished, he felt satisfied. The others at the table looked impressed, or somehow stunned by his satisfaction with the grub. Once the trays and utensils were collected by more kitchen staff they lined up again, and were led back to the block.

Eddie decided to go into the day room but when he saw that no guard was around, he turned and started back to his cell. Suddenly he was grabbed from behind, and pushed violently into an empty cell. He managed to stay on his feet. There were three of them including a crazed, snarling Gutz. His right bloodshot eye was twitching, the skin around it black, and yellowish. The other two held Eddie firmly.

"Now pretty boyo we're gonna show you how a bitch boyo is treated in heah." He showed Eddie a little tube of Vaseline, and grinned exposing crooked, stained teeth. Then a number of things seemed to happen almost at once. There was a sound, Eddie slammed his heel onto one of his captor's toes. He let go long enough for Eddie to slam an elbow into the other's chin. He was such a bear-like hulk, it barely affected him. But then Gutz was saying: "W-w-w wait Saul!" and "W-w-wait Jimmy." And they saw that Max was holding a wicked looking shiv, (a razor securely tied to a toothbrush handle) to Gutz's throat. Gutz was immobile with fear. Max said:

"The next time you clowns try a stunt like this I will slit each of your throats, and bleed you out. Or Eddie and me might take turns kicking your stupid skulls in." Eddie shoved the slighter Jimmy over into the arms of Saul who had his big, mouth hanging open and a dull idiotic look on his face. Gutz said:

"O-o-o-okay Max, okay you. Truce. We all gotta live here I guess. Okay I fucked up. I fucked up!"

Max shoved him toward his two road hogs and he and Eddie stepped backwards out of the cell. Three black convicts were standing nearby, and Max gave them a nod and they moved on.

Eddie said, "Much obliged, for literally saving my ass."

They both laughed.

In the day room Eddie sat with Max and talked. Another con joined them who seemed very interested in Eddie. Max told him to fuck off. There was a communal sink in the room. A little later they became aware that this same guy was washing his prick in it. He went on, and on. The cons started complaining, until finally two guards came in, and dragged the nut case away. Another event was when the overt homosexual and drag queen cell block was taken to chow separately. It was as though a group of showgirls had suddenly entered the prison. The cons made catcalls, kissy noises, that were obviously appreciated by the passing group. Max said: "Fuckin' cons. Fuckin' queers."

A trustee wearing an eye patch wheeled the library cart up to D Block. Eddie joined the others, and picked out a well thumbed Rex Stout. Max asked Eddie if he would like to rent a porno book. Eddie asked if it was any good. Max said he could get him one, but couldn't vouch for its quality. About then a guard stepped into the room and called Eddie over. He said his street clothes were in his cell, and told him to get dressed. Max joined him in his cell.

"You're getting out, slick. They don't give you your street threads for any other reason. Believe me, I've been in and out of this joint long enough to know."

"I hope you're right, but I think it's to take a polygraph."

"No, man, you won't be coming back. It would be a first. Even if you was going to court, you'd be given a red jumpsuit, see."

Max rubbed his chin with a big hand, and smiled with his eyes. He said:

"And I'd like a little favor if you would?"

"Of course Max, what?"

"Fly me a kite." He showed him a small piece of paper that had printing on it so tiny one would need a magnifying glass to read it.

"It's to my girlfriend." He carefully looked over Eddie's clothes. He took his jacket, cut a slice with his shiv in the black and white swirl lining on the black part. He inserted the tiny paper, and placed a minute piece of scotch tape behind the cut. He showed Eddie that it was impossible to see.

"Besides," Max said; "They barely search you going out, just your pockets, and a basic pat. You'll get your shoes, belt, watch and shit later."

Max had Eddie repeat his girlfriend's name and address until he was sure he had it memorized.

"Screw," Max said under his breath seeing the approaching guard. Eddie shook his hand.

"I wish you luck Max."

"Be sure to send me some cigarette money when you can."

The guard said:

"Let's go Knox. Kiss your boyfriend goodbye now."

They laughed and Max patted Eddie's shoulder as he went off with the guard.

20

The release was more of a formality. The guards who conducted it were friendly, gave Eddie a cup of real coffee, (only weak tea was served in chow). They joked with him, one even kicking back in his chair with his feet up. There was a knock and an odd priest entered. He was around forty, clean shaven, with shiny skin, wide glasses, and blond slightly unkempt hair. He had a stiffness about him, as though he was made of wooden parts rather than flesh and bone.

"You Knox?" he asked.

"I am. Am I to be executed, father?"

The guards laughed. The priest did not, only muttering something under his breath about blasphemy. One of the guards said:

"Oh Father, he's okay, but if you'd rather not take him we can provide the usual transportation."

The priest looked Eddie over.

"No, I'll take him. Maybe I can teach him something on the way."

It was explained to Eddie that Father Murphy would provide a ride to his appointment with the Feds. "I want him cuffed" said the wooden priest. The guard said hokay, and proceeded to cuff Eddie. Sadists in every profession, he thought, steeling himself to get along with this creep the best he could.

The priest drove a crappy car that smelled vaguely of feet. Eddie asked if he could have the window cracked. The priest ignored him. Eddie felt he wasn't off to a good start. He tried to concentrate on the passing scenery, fields, farmhouses, roadside stands, apple orchards, and more empty fields. When they turned onto a freeway, the priest finally spoke:

"I ought to take this collar off and beat you to a pulp for what you said back there." He turned to Eddie with a face full of rage, and a psychotic look that scared the hell out of him. He was convinced the man was unbalanced, disturbed, and he had no way to protect himself.

"I apologize father. Being locked up does funny things to you, and I just wasn't thinking."

"Do you know how many men I've given the last rites to? No, how could you, young punk that you are. Only last year a man that I know to be innocent, certainly innocent in the eyes of God was taken from this world by the almighty State. What gives them that right? Oh sure they've stopped it now, but for how long?"

Eddie kept quiet, hoped his apology had some effect but when an uncomfortable silence prevailed he thought he would try to add to it, test the waters:

"Father, I agree with you, the State has no right."

"Yeah, now you agree, now that you're handcuffed, my prisoner to do with what I want. Do you agree that I have the right to pick sinners who should be banished from this Earth too?"

Eddie figured that the priest had killed before. There was currently a serial killer targeting men around his age in Los Angeles. He wondered if this deranged priest could be him, or at least capable of being a copy cat.

"I can say you tried to escape, got out of your cuffs, and I had to defend myself. I have a pipe in the back seat I can use to bash in your skull after having some fun."

Eddie was seriously freaking out. The priest looked to be enjoying himself, and said:

"God works in mysterious ways."

Eddie heard the siren, Father Murphy said fuck! fuck! fuck! fuck! and pulled over. A moment later a trooper was at the window asking for his license, registration. Eddie didn't hesitate.

"Officer this maniac has threatened to murder me!" He showed him the cuffs. "Shut the fuck up!" Father Murphy snapped.

"Officer I'm being transferred. Could you follow us please?"

The trooper took off his sunglasses, demanded that they both get out of the car. Another trooper chewing gum joined them, and they were each talked to separately. Eddie watched Murphy showing the other policeman the transfer paperwork. Eddie said:

"Listen officer, help me. He's a psychopath. Maybe he's even the serial killer you're looking for. He said he'd kill me, and report it as an escape, or self defense. Could you take me to the interview? I'm to take a polygraph with the FBI, agent Nelson Sheldon. Today!" The two troopers conversed out of range. Eddie watched rubber neckers slow down, and look at the mad priest who glared back at them, flipped the bird at one. The second trooper went back to the cruiser, used the radio. When he strode back he brought everyone together.

"Father Murphy, we will follow you, and escort you to the transfer of this prisoner. That way everyone is happy, and that's what the Feds want."

Father Murphy said that was bullshit. He looked to be grinding his teeth. Eddie felt the relief complete now. He got back into the car, the trooper who was smiling, chewing gum, opened the door for him. Father Murphy didn't say another word until he parked behind the pyramidal Federal building. The cruiser parked behind them.

"You don't know how lucky you are. I was gonna slice you up into thin strips and cook myself a crunchy meal."

"Charming," Eddie said as his door opened. There stood agent Sheldon wearing a black turtleneck, black jeans, and black cowboy boots.

"Good to see you again Mr. Knox. I think we can put an end today to your incarceration and any further detention. Again I apologize for the inconvenience, but you know this is federal, and we are all slaves to that special bureaucratic entity and its processes."

Agent Sheldon told the priest to uncuff Eddie, and scolded him for having them on in the fist place. One of the troopers took Sheldon over to the side and spoke to him out of range of the others. Sheldon was nodding his head and listening. Sheldon waved everyone forward with a manila folder.

"Off we go gentleman. Let's get this done now."

After two security checkpoints both Eddie and Father Murphy signed release forms at a window. Father Murphy went on his way along with the two highway patrol officers. Eddie didn't like cops, but he had to thank those two, and he did before they left. Father Murphy gave him one last venomous look. The gum chewing trooper caught it and shot Eddie a glance saying he'd seen it too. Agent Sheldon opened a wide door, held it, said to Eddie with a smile:

"Shall we?"

They walked out onto a glassed in bridge that overlooked a vast room full of activity below: gray metal desks, old file cabinets, mostly men, some on phones, some women too. Eddie stopped, Sheldon did too. The scene below was right out of the forties/fifties noir or hard-boiled era. Eddie wondered if he'd somehow stepped into another time travel script. The men wore double breasted suits, with elaborate ties, suspenders, and cocked back fedoras. Some smoked cigars. The ladies were dames, femme fatales, with pointed bras and seamed stockings. What was this? This was Hollywood but—

"An experiment that I'm not at liberty to discuss," said Sheldon taking Eddie's arm in a friendly manner, and leading him away. They boarded an industrial elevator that smelled faintly of oil. It seemed to descend forever, giving Eddie a slight feeling of nausea. It clanked to a stop and they stepped out into a vast room. The lighting created a spooky mood. In the center stood a gray leather chair on a stage. Eddie thought it looked like a ultra modern dental chair, or what a commander of some space mission might use. Dim bluish lights pulsed from high above. Also on the stage were a black desk, a fantastic looking machine out of a science fiction story and to the side, some enlarged prints of the few snap shots Eddie had taken around Mexico City. Agent Sheldon patted the machine and said:

"The Truth Force 3611. It's flawless and benign. So chase away any fears that you've aroused. After you've been wired to it for five minutes we'll know if you're telling the truth, which I believe you are. We can also see the locations on a computer map of places you've been in the last week but were not aware of. So, shall we?" Sheldon gestured for Eddie to proceed to the chair. Sheldon sat at the desk, opened the folder. He began making adjustments on a console and typing on a keyboard. A grinding sound emerged that softened to a hum.

"Just climb up there and get comfortable," said Sheldon dreamily, "...that's all you have to do."

Eddie stepped up, and tried not to think about it. He reclined in the space chair. He knew from Dr. Kublar that the power cave location would not show up. A clear cover slowly began to descend from above. Sheldon said: "Stay still, it's harmless." And then Eddie was entombed, but before paranoia and suffocation fantasies could overwhelm him, he felt a jab in his buttocks. He flinched, and protested, but then it was like a black door was slammed shut. Eddie was lost to the sudden fierce winds of some strange void. He went out. When he came to he was still in the chair. The cover gone, and agent Sheldon standing there looking at him, and biting on the end of a pen.

"Okay Knox, you check out. I have a new plane ticket for you back to San Francisco. I can only warn you about your relationship with Dr. Kublar or anyone else associated with him. We consider him a highly suspicious character. Although we haven't arrested him for anything yet, we keep a close watch. And that goes for anyone who has dealings with him. I'm telling you this for your own good."

Without his glasses agent Sheldon squinted, and with a creepy smile offered a hand which Eddie waved off. He stood and stretched.

"Perhaps you'd consider working for us? For your country? Reporting on Kublar's activities? It would pay quite well."

"No thank you, but I will take your other advice," Eddie said as they stepped down from the stage. "This has all been too freaky for me. I want to get back to my own interests, writing, music, maybe some more travel but not this kind of travel."

"I see. Well, okay, let's go then. I'll give you a ride to the airport. I have your bag," Sheldon said, handing him back his photographs, but keeping the enlargements.

Agent Sheldon drove a silver 1953 Oldsmobile right out of the noir police facade/set Eddie had viewed earlier. He was tempted to ask Sheldon if his nickname was The Phantom, but he didn't want to annoy him in any way. The car was a wonder though, and obviously souped up. It moved down the freeway in a silver/gray blur like some kind of a ghost racer. Eddie said wow and far out a couple of times. Sheldon turned off, down a back road, then another of dirt. They stopped before Eddie could give it much thought. He gave Eddie a shitty smile, and showed him a snubbie he'd snatched from an open shoulder holster.

"What's the idea?"

"Sorry Knox, but you had your chance to do the right thing,

and you failed. It's time now for the walk.

"Out!"

Eddie obeyed, looking around: on his side was a wooded area, the other side wild brush that led up a hillside.

"Down the road Knox!" Sheldon poked him with the gun. Eddie thought he would crack his skull into Sheldon's at the kill spot, then use his legs as weapons as Dr. Kublar had taught him, but realized it was iffy. Then he noticed something moving in the foliage, like when you see an animal that has been camouflaged coming into focus: It was Mu. He put a blow gun to his lips. Sheldon put a hand to his neck, said fuck, and looked at Eddie. His eyes fluttered, and he went down.

"Boy am I glad to see you," said Eddie to the quick moving Mu.

"We take him back to car prease."

And they did, and put him in the driver's seat. Mu said he would be right back. A few minutes later Dr. Kublar's old Buick pulled up behind. Mu took a machine the size of a bread box out of the trunk. It came with a headband made of copper and leather that held tiny tubes. He fitted it onto agent Sheldon's head. Mu turned some dials, flipped a switch making some bleeps, the tubes pulsed red. Eddie watched Sheldon's face muscles contort and stretch like he was breaking the sound barrier.

"Brain machine. When he wakes he forgets you. Dr. Kublar will fix you with new ID, new everything. We drive back now. Pacific Coast Highway, verly slow, verly nice. But first show you somethink."

Eddie followed Mu down the dirt road, then down a path that led to a low, foreboding gray cement building with a slanted roof. Mu opened the door with Sheldon's key, and flipped on a light. Eddie had his first look at a human incinerator, a crematorium, a furnace for humans.

"We only kill when must. We could put him here, where he

wished for you, but brain machine better, since no more investigation. Dead track."

"Dead track?"

"Case crowsed. Even he saw you, wouldn't see you."

"Wouldn't recognize me?"

"Yes, Mister Edward."

When they returned agent Sheldon was leaning against the door, slumped forward, a string of drool hanging from his open mouth.

"When will he come to?"

"Soon soon. I get Brainer and we leave."

Eddie remembered the note he was to deliver for Max. He told Mu about it. A half hour later Eddie was knocking on a door of an apartment in a ghetto neighborhood, getting curious looks from folks in other windows and lurking on dimly lit corners nearby. A pretty black woman in very short shorts and bare feet answered the door. She frowned at Eddie as though he was some bad news. She put a hand on her hip like she was ready to deal with whatever it was. Eddie asked her if she was Tania and handed her the note. He said it was from Max and her suspicious look turned friendly. She stepped outside, gave him a hug, a peck on the cheek, then another hug.

Eddie enjoyed the scenic drive back, the silence of Mu, the warm security and plushness of the old car, and soothing ocean vistas passing them by. Later Eddie asked Mu how he had tracked him. Mu explained that the doctor had spies within the government, and knew where Eddie was at all times. After a stop for some forgettable grub Eddie climbed into the back for a snooze. Mu drove on, softly singing an old Chinese folk song to himself....

21

Back in San Francisco Eddie joined Dr. Kublar on the roof under a brilliant blue and yellow tarp for tea and biscuits. The air was cool, but the sun appeared, promising to warm the day. It felt good to Eddie after the humidity, and stale air of the jail. He told the doctor about the entire trip in much detail. Dr. Kublar was dressed in a white robe with a hood that came to a peak. He looked to be almost glowing in the early morning light.

Although Eddie was eager for more conversation, he learned that Dr. Kublar and Mu would be leaving for a month's return to Tibet. Eddie would be left in charge of the building. He would have a list of duties that included letting a cleaning woman in once a week to dust. He would bring in the mail, feed and tend to Robo, a tiger-striped house cat who would later move in with him, and sleep at the foot of his bed. Dr. Kublar recommended that Eddie continue his writing, explore solitude, practice what he'd learned so far and find The Other. But he didn't elaborate what he meant by that. Dr. Kublar said his apartment was available for Eddie to use and suggested a daily meditative walk through the rooms at the very least.

"Keeps the spirits content, you know."

"Are you concerned that the Feds are watching you?"

Dr. Kublar laughed. "The poor men don't know what they're watching. What they see is not what is happening. It's amusing

Edward, nothing more. When agent Sheldon looks at new photographs or footage of you he will not recognize you. And even if he is presented with your mug shot and jacket, he'll be convinced you are someone else. And you will be. You'll have a new ID. In another week they will drop the entire investigation."

On the first day without Dr. Kublar and Mu, Eddie woke to a scratching on his door. He found Robo sitting there, his eyes flashing with magical intensity. Eddie threw on a robe, stepped into house slippers, and trudged upstairs to the kitchen nook. Robo followed. He fed the cat, and took a look at the litter box. He took out a couple of turds with a scooper, bagged it, and dropped the bag drop down the garbage chute on his way back to his place. He designed a schedule for himself that included writing, exercising, relaxing, focused deep breathing, sun bathing, drinking plenty of mineral water, and being mindful that everything was in the best balance he could place it. Overall Eddie felt pretty good, and productive. He was getting close to a state he'd often longed for. He sifted through his adventures in a meditative state, starting with when he'd fled Pennsylvania nearly five years ago. He explored the fantastic teachings of Dr. Kublar and marveled at the many otherworldly events that had marked their relationship. It seemed too much to comprehend. He was still transforming. Dr. Kublar explained it, saying he would find a comfortable level in time, but always be in transition, always learning, and ultimately teaching. One thing that was curious to Eddie was that despite his extraordinary experiences and present state of mind, he found that his thoughts kept wandering back to someone else:

Alice....

22

Downtown. Eddie stopped at a record shop to see what was new. Occupying an entire display rack was Wolf Snake's self-titled first album. The band's name was in white ancient Greek style lettering on a black shiny background. Eddie bought it, and booked time in a listening booth. He put the head phones on. The back of the jacket was identical with the tracks listed there in white. And there was "Love Driver" and there was Knox alongside Turner and Coleman, as well as listed under backup vocals. He opened the gatefold cover to find a collage of snapshots, and hand printed notes and lyrics. At the top was an elegant drawing of a cavern occupied by a huge serpent, a wolf, and a voluptuous Persephone. He found a photo of himself in the studio singing, wearing headphones, with his eyes shut, and another of him on a couch with Richmond toasting with beer bottles. Below was a dedication to the three who had died in LA. He was finding the sound of the record to be incredible. The producer had found that sweet spot that was just enough production to make it accessible to most ears, yet maintaining the rawness and energy of the band that so appealed to their passionate hard core fans. A tap taping on the window at first annoyed him. But when he saw who it was, all was forgiven. He left the booth, joined a smiling and fresh looking Alice, her hair now long with bangs. She gave him a big hug, and a kiss. Eddie felt a warm rush of excitement. He thought she looked excited to see him.

"I was just thinking of you the other day," said Eddie. "Do you have time for a coffee?"

She said she had about a half hour left before she had to get back to work. She served cocktails in the Terrace Room at the Saint Francis hotel. They settled for coffee at a diner, and sat at the counter. She looked over the collage inside the LP.

"I'm in there. Can you find me?" She asked.

Eddie looked again, zeroed in on a small black and white of Alice with a guy who looked something like Brian Ferry, although blond with rockabilly sideburns.

"That's Brad, my so called boyfriend. He came here to join the band, the Stingers."

"Why so called?" Eddie asked, immediately feeling his hopes being dashed.

"Oh, I don't know. I'm not good with relationships. It all starts well, then you start taking each other for granted. You magnify the short comings, or even worse, you begin demanding behavior, according to some unwritten and unrealistic going together code. Are you involved at all? Have you been?"

"No. There was a childhood romance that I ended abruptly when she showed up one day in an outfit I found so brash and unbecoming I felt physically ill. No fashion sense. That was it. And last year I was dumped by a coed in Berkeley for a jock."

Alice laughed, and put her hand on Eddie's arm to steady herself. They looked into each other's eye's for a lost moment.

"Are you still seeing Amanda?"

"What? No, we only went out once."

"No follow up?"

"Nope, I never called her back, and she never called me. Wasn't meant to be."

"You never called me either. Why?"

"Because I'm an idiot."

Alice gave him a sweet smile.

"What do you want to do, Eddie? I mean with your life?" she asked studying the collage more.

"Hmm-mm, well, I want to continue writing. I've had a taste of travel, and I'd like to do more. Spain, Greece, North Africa — spend a year or so moving around Mediterranean ports."

"Yes, me too!" she said locking eyes with him again.

"We could go together."

"There's a little thing called money honey. We could rough it I guess. Teach English or something?"

Eddie's hopes were rekindled.

"Money is not a problem," he said.

She gave him a look.

"Really? I didn't realize you were loaded. What, did you rob a bank?

"I wanna study photography Eddie. I start a six week course next week. I've been told I'm good. I've had an interest since I was a kid. Now I wanna get serious. Maybe I'll, um use you as a model."

She looked at her watch, and said: "Do you still go to the Cabaret?"

"I haven't. I've been leading a different routine: early to bed, early to work on my book, sticking to a certain schedule that I told you about before. Weekends are pretty much the same. You?"

"Not so much, but I remember you being a good dancer. I'd go to dance with you."

Eddie's hopes went up another notch, and he offered to walk her back to work. They left the diner. She took his arm as they walked up Powell Street, past the packed cable cars near Union Square. As they approached the Saint Francis Eddie asked:

"So, what night shall we dance?"

"Saturday night around ten then?"

"It's a date, but will Brad be coming?"

Alice frowned for a second: "'Fraid so. He barely lets me outta his sight. Part of the problem..."

"And he won't be annoyed with me?"

She laughed, sang: "John, I'm only danc--ing."

Eddie knew the next lines were: "She turns me on. Don't get me wrong."

"But will you tell him our history?"

"Of course not."

She gave him a hug, and when she went to kiss his cheek he turned quickly so it landed on his mouth. He held her there, kissing her more. She didn't pull away. When she finally did, she tweaked his nose and gave him a half-scolding look. He watched her walk through the revolving glass doors. Eddie walked back to Chinatown through the Stockton tunnel with thoughts of Alice circling his brain. He was walking on air after the kisses, and the look she'd given him.

Saturday night at the Cabaret was a different story. He wasn't sure if he would go. Take out in Union Square with Alice on her lunch hour sounded far better. But was it some kind of a test? And if he didn't show, would that be it? Alice was a strange one. Even though she had settled some, this could still be a deciding moment for her. Forget Alice, Eddie was thinking. Women in general were impossible to know, part of the appeal really: The Other!

"Find The Other" the doctor had said....

23

Saturday night came and Eddie decided not to go, but rather to stick to his schedule. He could catch Alice at the hotel in the light of day, and see what was what. But when he put his headphones on after a late Chinese dinner and lit a joint, he began obsessing about her: reliving fun times with her, conversations, sleeping with her. He imagined her looking for him at the Cabaret. Maybe Brad hadn't even made it for some reason. Other possibilities ran through his head until he pulled off the headphones, dressed, and went out. He would be a half hour late. Big deal, he thought looking at his reflection in a store window, and running a hand through his hair that had recently been cut much shorter by a non-English speaking Chinese barber. The style reminded him of his juvenile delinquent days.

The club was packed, noisy, and sweaty. Although he loved the music loud, tonight it bothered him. He was feeling out of sorts as he made his way through the crowd. He was regretting his decision to come when he ran right into her.

"Eddie! Hey let's go. Let's get out of here. I can't stand it." The last two sentences she said into his ear. Eddie thought she smelled wonderful. Outside it felt good as they walked along Broadway under the neons, by the landmarks: Enrico's, the Condor, Big Al's. They were both unusually quiet, only making slight attempts at chit chat. Across the street a lanky figure kept stopping and looking over at them, then proceeding, not too far behind. At

City Lights Bookstore they looked at titles in the window. Alice said: "One day your book Eddie."

"I doubt it'd be in the window, but I'll settle for it being on the shelf."

"What's it about anyway?"

"Well, it's a work of fiction, fantastic fiction actually and it concerns a most mysterious man, who is part Tibetan. He leads the main character into the world of the occult, into an alternate world really. Living here in Chinatown has been very helpful in making the story come to life for me. I don't want to tell you much more, as to spoil it."

"I'll bet it's amazing Eddie. I can't wait to read it."

Eddie noticed a button she was wearing and was startled to see it said: The Guardians.

"What is that? Who–?"

"A new band from London. You'd love them."

They approached Chinatown. Eddie asked if she would like to see where he lived.

"Dont'cha wanna know why Brad wasn't with me?" She said.

"Sure."

Alice punched his arm.

"Don't be coy with me. You're dying to know."

"I'm dying to kiss you...all over."

She laughed. "Then I'll need another drink!"

They went into a little bar in Chinatown. Alice told him that she'd broken up with Brad, and that it had been coming for some time. She said that he'd gone psycho and showed Eddie two ugly bruises on her arm. "One on my leg too." She rolled down a knee high stocking to show him. She started to sniffle. Eddie held her, and told her she was smart to get away, that Brad had better hope that he didn't cross his path. Eddie went out of his way to avoid fights, but he would make an exception for this one.

"Alice, after your photography course I want you to come with me to Europe and North Africa. We'll go to London first. We'll see the Guardians!"

"I think I'd go anywhere with you."

"Why don't I get you home now. You can see my place another time."

"No, Eddie, now," she pleaded. "I want to come over now. I want us to take this new drug together: ludes, Quaaludes I have some."

Eddie laughed, and said sure. They went on their way. He took pleasure in showing her the back alleys he so loved in Chinatown, telling her some history as they walked along, all to take her mind elsewhere.

"Yes, Eddie, I love it too."

They stopped and watched a couple of lion dancers shaking madly. An older Chinese couple banged on cymbals, another a drum, and a gong. A kid set off strings of fire crackers. Some traditional Chinese music came from a shop. A string of paper lanterns hung above the street. They walked on, and entered an alleyway with black fire escapes climbing the side of brick buildings, festooned with hanging laundry. Brad stepped out of an alcove knocking into a trash can. He was either drunk or nervous, or both. Alice said oh fuck, and Eddie had her stand aside against the brick wall by a closed up flower shop. Brad went into a kind of wrestler's crouch, flicked open a switchblade. Alice yelled: "You're an asshole!"

Brad took a step forward. Eddie did too, and now he could clearly see the brown roots growing out under Brad's platinum hair, his green eyes. Eddie swiped his trusty Buck knife from his boot in a lightning move. He twirled it. Brad flinched. The knife was a permanent part of Eddie's city wardrobe. It made Brian's blade look like a joke. The Buck knife reflected light from a overhead street lamp and appeared like some potent magical weapon there: Excaliberesque. Eddie felt flooded with strength and confidence. Brad's mood looked to have shifted to uncertainty. His expression fearful, and his eyes starting to shift. Eddie, a stone faced warrior, showed teeth, and stepped forward in a slight crouch. He swiped the air with his blade and laughed. Brad turned and ran, but not fast enough to miss a swift kick in the back side sending him crashing into a parked car. He got to his feet, panic all over his bruised face. He had dropped his blade, but didn't go back for it. Instead he made like a 100 yard sprinter. Eddie picked it up and put it away. An old Chinese man dressed in a gray cloak, wearing long chin whiskers was passing, glanced at him, muttered something, continued on.

"He deserves more," Eddie said to Alice who was now hugging him. Eddie was pumped with adrenaline. They held each other for a while.

"Let's go now." Eddie said. "My pad is right around the corner."

About the author

Johnny Strike is an American writer, who William S. Burroughs praised with: "These are real maps of real places. That is what makes the artist. He has been there and brought it back"
Headpress published Strike's first novel in 2004, *Ports of Hell*. He has interviewed Paul Bowles, Mohamed Choukri, Herbert Huncke and traveled, with extended stays in Morocco, Mexico and Thailand, where he set his fiction.

His writing has appeared in *Ambit Magazine*, *Headpress Journal*, *Si Señor*, and *Pulp Adventures*. His short story collection, *A Loud Humming Came From Above*, was published by Rudos and Rubes in 2008. Richard Sala, a popular artist, provided the accompanying illustrations.

He is also known as a songwriter, guitarist and singer for the proto-punk band Crime, based in San Francisco. *Naked Beast* is his latest music endeavor with Guitars and Bongos. His novel *Murder in the Medina* follows another Tangier mystery, *Name of the Stranger*, both published by Bold Venture Press.

Never get involved with a patient ...
especially not if the patient
is Robert Sutherland ...

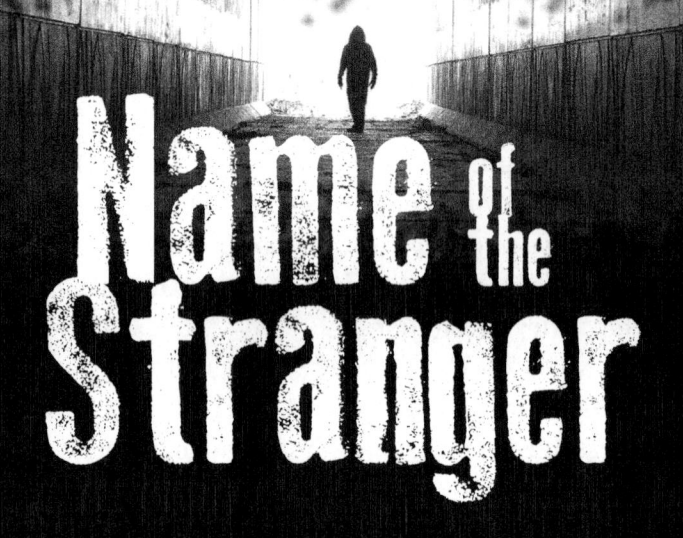

Name of the Stranger

A contemporary suspense thriller by

Johnny Strike

BOLD VENTURE

In modern Tangier, expat artists are targeted by a diabolical cult. Enter the djinns …

Murder in the Medina

A weird-menace thriller by

Johnny Strike

www.boldventurepress.com

Continuing series from Bold Venture Press ...

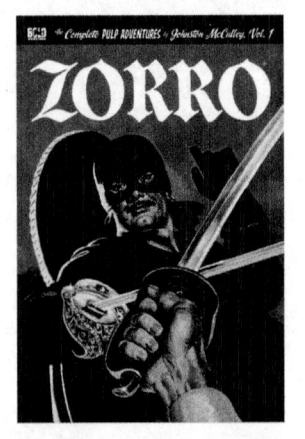

Zorro: The Complete Pulp Adventures
Six volumes by Johnston McCulley
In the early 1800s, California was still under Spanish rule. Some of the military commanders plundered and won riches at the expense of the peace-loving settlers. Against these agents of injustice, the settlers were powerless, until one man arose whose courage inspired Californians and gave them the spirit to resist tyranny. That man was Zorro!

The Cathedral *by TJ Morris*
His given name was But for the Love of Jesus Christ We Would All Be Damned Smith, III; BC for short. He was the best enforcer in service of The Church, the governing force controlling the interstellar harvest of resources. Then he developed a conscience, and all Hell broke loose. *The Cathedral* combines high-concept speculation and cliffhanger thrills.
First in the "Cleanser" series

Pulp Adventures
Audrey Parente, editor
Every issue is a voyage across the landscape of pulp fiction — mystery, science fiction, horror, romance, western, and more! from lush jungles to sun-baked deserts, lawless wild west towns to utopian cities of the future! Don your pith helmets and fedoras and embark on great reading!

www.boldventurepress.com